A VISIT TO LONDON

"On my last two visits to London I have been quite shockingly bored," said Mr. Develyn.

Francesca glanced up and laughed. "Let us hope," she said with a gleam of wicked mirth, "that in my efforts to prove entertaining, I do not set Society by the ears—as you must be aware I am accustomed to doing."

There was a hint of challenge in the last remark, despite the airy nonsense. He met it equably. "Let us agree that you are an abandoned hussy and quite past praying for, shall we? If you choose to create riot and rumpus, it is very much your own affair."

She grinned. "Nonsense! I'll wear sober gowns and even a cap if you like. Everyone will think I'm your maiden aunt and we'll brush through with never a hint of scandal."

STRANGER WITHIN THE GATES

Mira Stables

A FAWCETT CREST BOOK

Fawcett Books, Greenwich, Connecticut

STRANGER WITHIN THE GATES

A Fawcett Crest Book reprinted by arrangement with Robert Hale
& Company

ISBN: 0-449-23402-9

Printed in the United States of America

10 9 8 7 6 5 4 3 2 1

For Jo

STRANGER
WITHIN THE GATES

One

Mr. Develyn watched the fourgon pull out of the inn yard with an appreciative eye for the well-muscled team that Gibb had selected for this arduous task. His overnight bag was carried down by the porter and added to the pile of well-worn luggage already stowed in the chaise. A silk-smooth head nudged his wrist and a pair of eloquent amber eyes were lifted yearningly to his. He caressed the boarhound's head absently, watching the chaise roll out of the yard in the wake of the fourgon. Ten o'clock. Even at the pace of the slower moving vehicle they should reach Saxondene before dusk.

The day was beginning to warm up a little. Mr. Develyn, accustomed for some years now to suns considerably warmer than those of an English September, stretched himself gratefully in its gentle benison and decided that he would ride rather than drive. If memory served him right it could be no more than fifteen or sixteen miles across country—a first-rate opportunity to try out his new hunter. There was just the shadow of doubt about the wisdom of that extravagant purchase. A handsome head and well set-on shoulders that no one could fault, and by the look of those powerful quarters he could leap anything that they were likely to encounter in this sort of country. But was he a trifle short in the back? Had he allowed his preference for a chestnut to lead him astray? To be sure, despite his name, Rustic's manners were perfect. Henshawe had vowed that a child could ride him. But it might be that he was short on staying power. Yes, Gibb should drive the curricle and he himself would essay Rustic's performance.

"But not you, my girl," he addressed the hound severely. "Not till you've learned English manners. We had enough of your barbaric behaviour yesterday."

Ears and tail sank in depression at the tone. The huge creature looked the picture of guilt. Mr. Develyn grinned. "Well—you were not to know the difference," he acknowledged kindly. "But until you have learned to distinguish between the domestic English sow and your hereditary enemy it will be both simpler and less expensive to keep you in leash. By the value he set on her, that sow must have been the prize specimen for the whole of Kent, though I agree with you that there was nothing in her appearance to justify such an assumption."

At this point his monologue was interrupted by the arrival of his curricle, Gibb fully occupied with the high spirited pair who appeared to be dancing in their eagerness for the open road.

"Keep 'em in hand," he called, as the groom drew

to a halt beside him. "And take Tara up with you. I'll
ride. Tell them at Saxondene I'll be there in time for an
early dinner. I've taken a fancy to visit the haunts of
my mis-spent youth. And it's the grand day that's in it
entirely for doing just that," he added provocatively.

Gibb maintained an impassive front. Master Robert
always adopted that exaggerated Irish lilt when he
wanted to tease. It made no odds. Irish the *Finmores*
might be, that dour man grudgingly admitted. The
Develyns—never! Mr. Robert Develyn—this Mr. Robert's father—might have seen fit to marry the Lady
Mary, sister of the Earl of Finmore, but he had been
born a Man of Kent and his sons likewise. Mr. Robert
was in spirits it seemed, and a pleasure it was to see him
so content in his native land. Gibb, for one, had had
more than his fill of foreign parts. Let Master Robert
just settle down in a decent Christian country where
a man could rely on the folk and the weather and
the ale being just as he expected, and Gibb would have
no complaints. He waited while his master stripped off
his long driving coat, tossed it up into the curricle, and
ordered the boarhound up beside him.

"It's my saddle that's on Rustic, sir," he reminded,
"and your own is away in the chaise with the rest of
your gear, seeing as how I thought you was meaning
to drive. But it fits him comfortably enough. You'll
do."

His employer nodded and waved him off, with a
recommendation that Tara should be fastened up upon
arrival lest she commit further crimes. He watched
the dashing departure of the light vehicle, the horses
settling to their work contentedly, Tara a melancholy
bronze statue beside the stolid Gibb, and turned back

in leisurely fashion towards the inn. For the first time in years he found himself well content to be in England, with no over-riding urge to be planning a new expedition, able to savour the beauty of a quiet countryside already touched by autumn's golden fingers and looking forward with a surprising degree of pleasure to an unexpected home-coming.

He had never thought to inherit Saxondene. And what had possessed the Earl of Finmore to leave it to him was a mystery that would never now be explained. He had not even been particularly well acquainted with his uncle though he had spent several holidays at Saxondene when the Earl had paid periodic visits to this very far-flung and insignificant portion of his vast estates and, as a boy, he had liked it very well. But it must be close on five and twenty years since last he had seen the place. He was pretty sure that he had still been at Harrow—and on his next birthday he would be forty. The mobile mouth twisted into a sardonic grimace. Perhaps it was the onset of old age that had so easily reconciled him to the abandonment of his nomadic existence!

He settled his reckoning, exchanged a few civil remarks with the landlord on the state of the weather and the weight and quality of the top harvest and strolled out again to the stable yard.

His new purchase looked even better than he had remembered. The lean, well-bred head turned to greet the ring of his footsteps, the ears flickering forward attentively. In the warm sunlight the chestnut hide gleamed and rippled over powerful muscles. The lad who had been left in charge of him was enthusiastic.

" 'E's a beauty, bain't 'e, sir? And kind with it," he

said reverently, running a loving hand from proud crest to shining withers. "Not a mite o' trouble 'e bain't."

Mr. Develyn nodded thoughtfully, his eyes acknowledging that, despite the obvious splendour, there *was* a doubt about that back. A coin slid into the boy's grubby fist as he surrendered the reins. Despite his advancing years Mr. Develyn swung lightly enough into the saddle, and Rustic walked sedately out of the yard.

At the end of an hour he was satisfied that he had not wasted his money. Rustic was a smooth easy ride with quite a pretty turn of speed. Nor had Henshawe over-praised his manners. He actually seemed to anticipate his rider's wishes so that only the merest hint with hand or heel was required to ensure his prompt co-operation. How he would stand up to a gruelling day's hunting over heavy country was yet to be seen, but in every other way he was all that a man could desire. Well pleased, Mr. Develyn let him drop to a walk and permitted himself to admire the countryside.

It was, admittedly, the country of his birth; of his earliest, happiest memories. Perhaps that accounted for its insidious appeal, for the unaccustomed sense of lazy well-being that soothed and drugged his normal restless energy. Or maybe—once more the thought crossed his mind—he was growing old. He smiled and shrugged. Well—at least he had an interest for his declining years, a comfortable down-setting for his ageing bones. There might even be archaeological discoveries to be made in Kent as absorbing, if less dramatic, as those that had taken him to Crete and Greece and Egypt and even as far as South America. Never was an inheritance so well timed, he thought cynically. There was something very suggestive about the bare hop poles standing lonely and undraped in the gardens, the hints of crimson and gold and brown that already touched the trees. A definite atmosphere of the sere and yellow.

His mood was unusual—but so were the circumstances. He had grown accustomed to living each day as it came. There had been no particular need to plan for a future, and at times—in Crete, for instance, in '21, there had seemed small likelihood that there would *be* any future. He recalled that on that occasion he had felt a certain degree of anxiety for his daughter's future. But financially she was well provided for, and what *could* a man do with a three year old daughter save leave her in the care of grandparents?

It had worked well enough, he reflected, giving Rustic the hint that a little more speed was required. Robin was eleven now, well grown for her age if rather pale and subdued. But that came of living in Town. A few months at Saxondene would soon put the roses in her cheeks, the animation in her bearing. Grandparents and a strict governess had suppressed her spirits more than he cared for, but that, too, could easily be mended.

The countryside was becoming more familiar. From time to time he passed a cottage—a crossroads—a stream that stabbed memory awake. He reckoned that he must be within two or three miles of Saxondene. At the crest of the gentle rise he checked Rustic and surveyed the prospect set before him. Away to the north was the sweep of the Downs, the rich mosaic of farmland and forest, of park and marsh held secure in their keeping, the lines of the sunken lanes that once had seen the passage of the heavy wagons carrying cannon for the fleet still deeply incised.

He took his bearings carefully. That would be Brenchley below him. He recognised the church. And far away to his right was Linton, perched on the very edge of the stone hills. He was almost home. He stirred Rustic to a gentle trot and went down the green ride that led to the turnpike. In his preoccupation with his mount he had deviated considerably from the direct route, but he remembered a short cut that would bring him out by the south lodge of Saxondene. Neither he nor Rustic cared for the turnpike and were thankful to abandon it for a farm track leading in the right direction. A convenient gap in a hedge admitted them to a stubble field but the hedge at the other side was both sturdy and thick. However it was no more than breast high and they had already cleared far stiffer obstacles with ease. Mr. Develyn set Rustic going, a little careless now, such was his confidence in the chestnut, with no thought for what might lie behind the hedge.

Too late he discovered his error. Beyond the hedge was a ditch, both deep and wide, the bank soggy and crumbling. Rustic had jumped big, but no horse can be expected to collect himself neatly when landing fetlock deep in a bog. He stumbled, recovered, and hauled himself into the lane, going dead lame on the near fore. Mr. Develyn slid from the saddle and stooped to assess the damage, cursing his own stupidity. Only an over reach, thank heaven, and no fault of the poor brute's. He had done well not to come down—and maybe a mud bath would have served his careless rider right. He fondled the drooping head and made much of him, explaining in the slow deep tones that he kept for Tara and his horses how it was that men had less than horse sense and must be pitied and tolerated by the nobler creation. He then proceeded to lead the limping animal slowly up the lane, expounding the while on the comfortable stable, the fresh straw, the warm mash that awaited the sufferer upon arrival, and thankful that he had made for the south lodge. The main gates of Saxondene faced east, and nearly a mile of winding avenue separated them from the stables, whereas the south lodge stood no more than two hundred yards from that desired haven.

He wondered idly if there was anyone living at the lodge. In his boyhood it had stood empty, a quaint whimsy of some long dead builder which looked more like a giant's pepper pot than a human habitation and offered much the same amenities as a mediaeval dungeon, being damp, dark and airless. Since the south entrance was rarely used save by vehicles delivering such commodities as hay and straw to the stables, his uncle had allowed it to fall into disuse. The gates generally stood hospitably open, and certainly were never locked.

But it was twenty five years since his last visit and he was to discover that many things were changed. Over the high wall that bounded the park at this point he could see several chimney stacks. This was new. There had been no houses there in his day. And the gates—new ones, handsomely wrought in iron—were not only shut but locked. However they were furnished with a bell pull which proved to be in excellent working order. His vigorous tug produced a clangour that could not fail to arouse the sleepiest of gate keepers and no doubt some one from the new cottages was charged with the duty of attending to its summons.

He waited. Nothing happened. He surveyed the new south entrance with the disapprobation natural in one whose boyhood memories had been betrayed, though no sensible man could deny that the elegant gates and the sweep of well kept drive that curled away out of sight to his left were a vast improvement on the picturesque but useless lodge of his recollection.

But at least, in the old days, he had never been kept waiting outside he reflected, annoyance growing within him. And now that he was master here he would see that it did not happen again. No doubt the servants had grown slack during the months that had elapsed since his uncle's death. The gate keeper, at any rate, was in for a rude awakening.

He pulled the bell again, with a force that was promptly transmuted into imperious summons. Even Rustic tossed his head nervously, sensing his master's displeasure. A little way off a door slammed and a moment later a boy stepped out on to the drive and strolled towards the gate.

There was no sign of haste or penitence in that leisurely approach. Mr. Develyn allowed mounting annoyance to blind him to the fact that the newcomer did not look in the least like an estate servant. Tall and slightly built, coatless, in white shirt and dark pantaloons, he bore himself with an insolent grace that never stemmed from peasant stock. Mr. Develyn, more concerned for his horse than with such trivialities as these, brushed aside a hovering wasp that was irritating Rustic and said sharply over his shoulder, "Would it be asking too much of you to stir your stumps, you idle whelp? That is the second time that I have rung for admittance and I am in no mind to wait any longer upon your pleasure."

"And I am in no mind to open my gates to any ill-bred lout who has not even the manners to ask it pleasantly," was the prompt response.

Mr. Develyn's head came up with a jerk and he stared in amaze. The voice was undoubtedly feminine, low and musical despite its vibrant indignation, its accent as pure as his own. Was he dreaming, or fevered? For a moment he actually glanced anxiously about him, half afraid that he had made some ghastly mistake. Surely this *was* Saxondene? Yes. Of course it was. There was the oak tree that he had climbed as a boy, and there, though it was scarcely recognisable, was the old lodge itself, now transformed into some kind of summer house.

Then if *he* was in his right mind, the woman must be crazed. It was the obvious explanation. Who but a lunatic would walk abroad quite unashamed in male attire? And she seemed to have some peculiar notion that this was *her* house. He wondered whether he should try to humour her and persuade her to open the gate for him or beat an ignominious retreat and subject poor Rustic to the weary plod of the long way home.

While he still hesitated, the cause of his dilemma produced the key from her breeches' pocket and inserted it in the lock. "However, since I perceive that you have lamed your horse, I will open the gates for *him*. Why should the poor beast suffer for his master's discourtesy? It would seem that he has already suffered from lack of horsemanship."

The gates swung back smoothly, silently. Mr. Develyn glared at the impudent hussy who dared to outface him as she held the gate for him to lead Rustic through, standing in an attitude of exaggerated subservience that made him itch to slap her. There had been nothing crazy about *that* remark! He would dearly have loved to turn on his heel and reject her charity— but not at the cost of Rustic's suffering. And she was right, damn her, about his horsemanship.

His gaze swept her from head to heels with a suggestion of faint surprise, amusement, dismissal. Any modest female should have blushed and shrunk from so flagrant an assessment. This one gave him back glance for glance. Only when she had shown him exactly how little she valued his opinion did she lower her gaze deliberately to Rustic's near fore. She shrugged infinitesimally, sighed rather more obviously and then allowed an expression of patient boredom to obliterate all other emotion.

Mr. Develyn conceded defeat. He touched his hat stiffly, said, "Thank you, ma'am," rather as though the words had been racked out of him, and walked steadily up the drive, aware in every fibre of his being of the cool mockery of the gaze that must be bent upon his ignominious retreat. He could not even make haste. Faintly, behind him, he heard voices and, he fancied, laughter. The shameless Jezebel was probably recounting the tale of his humiliation. He gritted his teeth and trudged on stablewards, resolved that before many days were past there should be a further accounting.

Two

"I don't like it," said Geoffrey Thornish slowly.

His sister surveyed him with amused affection. He might like it as little as he pleased. The fact remained that there was nothing that he could do about it. But because she valued the loyalty that had brought him to visit her and guessed that in the face of all the circumstances the visit had demanded a certain degree of moral courage, she did not stress this undoubted truth.

Encouraged by her forbearance her brother went on, "It must have been awkward enough while the old Earl was alive, but even Aunt Maud admitted that of late he rarely visited Saxondene, though still she vowed that you was living under his protection and that it was an open scandal."

"And I daresay she hinted pretty broadly that my advancing years and fading charms were responsible for the infrequency of his visits," retorted his sister tartly.

He grinned. "That, of course. You've not forgot the way she has of cutting up a character in the meekest possible way! But I paid no heed. Why! Lord Finmore must have been eighty. However great a rake he may have been in his younger days, he must have been long past it when you met him."

Irrepressible amusement curved Francesca's mouth. Brothers could be so amazingly tactful! "I would scarcely say *that*," she said carefully. "He was by no means senile, you know, even at the end. You must blame my callowness rather than his decrepitude for the fact that our relationship was that of father and daughter. I was seventeen—by far too raw and ingenuous to appeal to such a noted connoisseur. Or so his lordship was kind enough to assure me at that momentous first meeting. And at the time *he* was but sixty five—and erect as a lance, with a vigour and gaiety that many a younger man might have envied."

The laughing eyes misted to the memory of the very great gentleman who had come to the aid of a desperate seventeen-year-old and had stood by her and sheltered her ever since. But he had straitly forbidden her to mourn, and he was a man whose commands must be obeyed, the more so, perhaps, that he was no longer there to enforce them.

Resolutely she smiled at Geoffrey, and then suddenly gave vent to a genuine chuckle as she said, "I fear he was a sad example to youth! Despite the excesses and follies of his early years he enjoyed excellent health—almost to the end. We travelled extensively, you know—first to Italy, because of my singing lessons, and much more widely thereafter. He was never weary, rarely out of temper, and savoured every minute to the full. Danger he loved. He said it added zest to living. But he was always very careful of *my* safety. And wherever we went I was hedged about with propriety. He had no sooner brought me to Saxondene than he engaged the Hornbys, and they have been with me ever since."

"Then what was all the fuss about?" asked Geoffrey, reasonably enough. "The man was old enough to be your grandfather. You were strictly chaperoned. So why should Aunt Maud insist that you were ruined?"

"Not because of my association with Lord Finmore," returned his sister quietly. "Oh no! *That* was on quite another count. Though it is true that it was his lordship whom Aunt Maud tried to coerce into marrying me with threats of the scandal she would create. Such stuff! Who would have suffered from a scandal? Certainly not the Earl of Finmore, with just one more affair added to his long tally, but the hitherto respectable if undistinguished Thornishes, suddenly illumined by a glaring notoriety. But Aunt Maud saw a heaven-sent opportunity in the circumstances that had brought the earl into my life and she never forgave me for my refusal to make the most of it. She might in time have come to see that I was not to be blamed for my abduction and the loss of my good name, but my crass stupidity in refusing to make a push to secure so fantastic a match was quite beyond her comprehension. She washed her hands of me."

Geoffrey looked more and more bewildered. "But if he abducted you, how can you say that he was like a father to you?" he enquired dazedly.

"Because it was not he who abducted me. I think I

had better begin at the beginning. It is so long ago, I forgot that you were only a schoolboy and would scarcely have heard the true tale. I suppose you were fobbed off with a tissue of half truths?"

"Aunt Emmy said I was not to mention your name in Aunt Maud's presence. You had behaved very badly, running off to Ireland with your lover just when all was in train for your presentation. It wasn't until Lord Finmore died that Aunt Maud let slip the fact that you were living here. I naturally supposed that it was Lord Finmore that you had run off with."

Francesca gave an exasperated sigh and shook her head. "No. In fact *he* is the only one who emerges from the episode with any credit. *I* was foolish and reckless, the aunts thought only of their position in society and Hugh O'Malley was an unprincipled adventurer."

"That the fellow that made off with you?"

She nodded. Looking back twelve years it was possible to be quite dispassionate about it. "He was very handsome, in the dashing military style," she said reflectively, "and very plausible. His manners were particularly charming. Aunt Maud was much taken with him. In fact he fooled us all completely. But though I enjoyed his company and liked having him gallant me to parties I was not in the least in love with him and he knew it. I suppose that was why he decided on abduction."

She fell silent a moment, thinking it over. Geoffrey shifted impatiently. His sister pulled a face at him. "I was quite a catch, you see," she informed him with demure mischief. "Young, biddable—or so he thought —and wealthy. And I suppose he had hopes of turning the aunts up sweet so that they, too, would remember me generously in their wills. I played into his hands when I consented to go with him to a display of fireworks at Vauxhall. At his suggestion I even bribed my maid to hide the fact that I was out! A great adventure I thought it, romantic little fool that I was. So of course there was no enquiry after me until it was too late."

"And then?"

"Oh—the coffee that he had given me was drugged. I woke up in a very shabby lodging in Liverpool to be informed that having passed two nights in his company there was nothing for it but marriage. He proposed to carry me to his home in Dublin and have the ceremony performed there. I am ashamed to confess that at first I could see no way of escape. You must forgive me for being so poor spirited. Remember that I was alone and penniless in a strange city with nothing but the clothes I wore—and sadly grubby and crumpled they were! Moreover I was feeling extremely unwell. It emerged that I had given my abductor a sad fright. The drug was stronger than he had thought and at one time he had entertained some doubts of my ever coming round. It was in this piteous condition that I allowed myself to be conveyed aboard the Irish packet. And then my luck turned. First the wind was foul and our sailing was delayed. The salt air did much to clear my numbed mind and I decided that *anything* would be preferable to such a marriage. So when my captor went off to play cards with some cronies he had met, thinking me safely laid upon my bed, I slipped out of the cabin intent on making my way ashore. That was when I met his lordship."

"He, too, was crossing by the packet?"

She shook her head. "No. I do not think he ever did so. When he was not riding or driving his beautiful horses, I think he was happiest at the helm of his yacht. It was the merest chance that had brought him on board—some matter of a horse that he wished to buy whose owner was returning to Ireland. He was on the point of going ashore when I emerged from my cabin and my furtive manner and dishevelled appearance aroused his curiosity. When I stumbled on the gang plank his hand was ready to catch me. He helped me ashore and asked if he should summon a carriage for me or escort me to my lodging since it was unwise for a young female to walk unprotected in the dock area. I don't know why I trusted him. Sheer desperation, perhaps, and his age and the air of calm dependability that informed his voice and bearing. I told him that I had neither money nor lodging, but that if he would help me I was well able to repay any expense that he incurred on my behalf."

"You took a grave risk," said Geoffrey soberly.

She smiled. "I know that—now. At the time it never entered my head that my benefactor might expect payment in a different coin. He accepted my appeal with perfect composure and suggested that we repair to his hotel to settle the details of the arrangement?"

"And you went? Without hesitation?"

"I did. And was handed into the care of a chamber maid who scolded and fussed as though she had been my nurse, tucked me into bed with a bowl of bread and milk for my supper, and presented me next morning with clean linen and a neat travelling dress and mantle that his lordship had sent her out to purchase for me. I was never so glad of anything in my life. You have no notion how horrid it is to be dirty and unkempt—let alone the impropriety of appearing at breakfast in my evening gown!"

"His lordship appears to have behaved with kindness and consideration," allowed her brother judicially.

Remembering that breakfast table encounter, Francesca chuckled. His lordship had been in a mind to repent of his overnight chivalry. By daylight, washed and combed and neatly dressed, Francesca had looked what she was—a gently bred child, scarcely out of the schoolroom. His lordship, who found respectable young ladies a dead bore, decided that honour would be satisfied if he hired a maid and a courier and despatched her, thus escorted, to the home and the anxious parents that he imagined for her.

She responded politely to his morning greeting, assured him that she had been perfectly comfortable and well attended, and then addressed herself to the consumption of a substantial breakfast without further remark. His lordship sipped hot coffee and regarded his waif with dawning amusement. Of all things he detested chattering females, especially at breakfast. But he was a man of considerable charm, and never before had he found himself of less account than a platter of grilled ham. A salutary experience, he decided.

He had to wait some time before his charge had satisfied the appetite induced by her long fast. Unobtrusively he studied her. Not pretty. Her mouth was too wide, her nose too dominant. But the eyes—when they were not bent on her plate—were very fine—a clear golden hazel, dark lashed and dark browed, and the hands that plied knife and fork so industriously were slender and graceful, the long fingers well kept. No rings, he noted automatically, and poured himself more coffee.

The silence between them was quite comfortable. The girl seemed relaxed and easy though she must be aware of his scrutiny. Yet there was nothing brash or offensive in her quiet composure. Quite an unusual young creature decided Lord Finmore, his interest now fairly caught.

He waited until she poured herself a second cup of coffee before he said gently, "And now, Miss Thornish, pray tell me how best I may be of service to you. If you care to explain how it came about that you were in so uncomfortable a predicament last night, I shall naturally respect your confidence. If you prefer to keep your own counsel, it remains only to arrange your journey home."

As he had confidently expected, the whole story came tumbling out. But there were no tears, no excuses, no appeal for sympathy. Rather there was indignation and a vengeful note in the warm young voice as she ended, "I suppose you will say that I was well served for my folly. I admit it. And I'll take good care I am never so cozened and tricked again."

The Earl's shoulders shook very slightly but he preserved an expression of grave interest. "Do you intend, then, to abjure society?" he enquired quizzically. "For I believe it is very difficult to detect the accomplished fortune hunter."

"As to that, it seems far more likely that society will abjure me," said the girl candidly. "But I was not thinking of that. I was planning rather that as soon as

I am back in Town I will engage a tutor to instruct me in the use of a pistol. If I can become a creditable shot—yes, and I would like to learn to handle a small sword as well—such gentry will think twice before they meddle with me."

For a moment she pondered this thought with obvious satisfaction, then turned to him with a smile of genuine sweetness, the golden eyes glowing with gratitude, and added, "I cannot expect a guardian angel to come to my rescue every time I behave foolishly."

The calm good sense of this practical appraisal of what was undoubtedly social disaster, coupled with the sudden vision of himself in the highly improbable role of guardian angel, overset the Earl entirely. A man who for years had prided himself on his complete imperturbability under all circumstances choked over his coffee and had to submit to being solicitously patted on the back. But having recovered from this minor mishap he established himself even more firmly in Miss Thornish's good opinion by murmuring thoughtfully that he might be able to assist her in finding just the sort of tutor she had in mind, but that meanwhile they had better decide when and how they would journey back to London. Gone was all thought of permitting this refreshingly unusual child to make the journey in charge of maid and courier. His lordship, amused and entertained as he had not been in months, had no intention of relinquishing his new acquaintance so easily.

By the time London was reached they were fast friends. They had travelled in leisurely comfort, taking four days over a journey that might well have been accomplished in half the time, since the Earl kept his own horses at each stage of a route that he used regularly in his comings and goings between London and his Irish estates. They had talked, intermittently but frankly, on whatever subject came into their heads. Miss Thornish, with a youthful resilience that compelled her companion's respect, appeared to have put from her all thought of her recent unpleasant experience and of the stormy reception that undoubtedly awaited her in London. He found her a delightful travelling companion, receptive and appreciative. She bore minor discomforts without fuss and told him frankly that travelling in the style that *he* maintained was a treat that she had never expected to enjoy and that she meant to make the most of it. She accepted his escort with a pretty courtsey and plainly enjoyed his company, calling his attention to anything that pleased or puzzled her. Her behaviour was modest without being foolishly coy, and despite the awkwardness of her situation she betrayed no trace of embarrassment.

Long before the Earl's travelling coach drew up in Cavendish Square, its noble owner was pretty well acquainted with Francesca's circumstances. He could have hazarded a shrewd guess as to how *his* presence would operate upon her aunts. And, being a man of sensitive perceptions, he had come to recognise the bitter loneliness that lay behind the girl's cool self-sufficiency. She had learned to depend upon herself because there was not one living soul who really cared for her happiness. Her younger brother was away at cshool, nor was he really of an age to understand her difficulties. Aunt Maud, self-centered and overbearing, thought only of social consequence. Aunt Emily, gently vague, simply closed her ears and eyes to anything that threatened her comfort. A niece who had created a resounding scandal would get little sympathy from either lady. In fact he felt it was fortunate for the girl that she was financially independent of her aunts.

Matters had fallen out much as he had anticipated. The shattering first encounter; the appearance of that meditative and calculating gleam in Aunt Maud's eye upon learning his identity; the hints let fall that the sinner might yet be received again into the virtuous precincts of Cavendish Square if her social credit could be re-established by the announcement of her betrothal. It was all of twelve years ago, but Francesca's mouth still curved distastefully at the memory of Aunt Maud's blatant opportunism.

"I fear the aunts were less easily convinced of my innocence than was his lordship," she said drily. "Having failed to ensnare an earl in her matrimonial net, Aunt Maud duly cast me out with every form of objurgation that she could lay her tongue to, short of actual anathema. Not even under *such* provocation could she bring herself to utter curses! His lordship then hurried me somewhat unceremoniously into Kent where he left me in his sister's charge until he had engaged the Hornbys to be my dragons. I was happy with the Lady Mary as I had never been in Cavendish Square. We were off on our travels within the month, but whenever our homecomings brought her to Saxondene I was always aware of that same well-being. She was the most warmly generous creature that I ever knew. One felt oneself liked, understood, accepted, faults and all. Yet she was never sentimental. Practical, comical, tender yet staunch. What a mother she must have been!"

There was a brief silence, a silence taut with unspoken thoughts. Then she went on slowly. "It is a pity that I discern no trace of that welcoming warmth in her son."

"Oh come!" exhorted her brother. "One unfortunate encounter! And both of you taken at a disadvantage." His glance flickered briefly, a little uneasily, over the male attire that this unconventional sister of his wore so casually. "You cannot so lightly condemn the poor fellow! Though as I said at the outset, I do not like it. Unlike his uncle, he, I take it, is to reside here permanently. To be living within a stone's throw cannot be comfortable for you. Surely some better arrangement can be made? If it's a question of the needful," he added awkwardly, "I'm pretty well inlaid. A snug little house in Tunbridge Wells, now, with the Assemblies and shops and libraries. Wouldn't that suit you better than this isolated spot? Comfortable as you have made it," he threw in hastily, belatedly remembering his manners.

"What! Permit myself to be turned out of my home? Just because my little brother has some absurd conventional notions carefully inculcated by Aunt Maud? No, my dear. You are very kind, but it would never do, you know. I wouldn't be received. Even here, where I am pretty well known, there is sometimes a little awkwardness, though I am fortunate enough to have a number of friends who are willing to take my morals on trust."

Geoffrey flushed up to the roots of his hair and looked so unhappy that she took pity on him.

"Now don't be thinking it distresses me. Only the stuffiest of the respectable matrons go so far as to give

me the cut direct—and I promise you I am much better
off without their acquaintance! As for my new landlord I daresay he will soon take himself off on his
travels again. He is a devoted amateur of antiquities,
you know. I daresay he has not spent as much as six
months in this part of the world since his wife ran off
with Mr. Ramsey."

"Ran off with—— I thought he was a bachelor!"

"Oh no! Divorced. There is a child—a little girl—
scarce out of leading strings, poor little scrap, when
her Mama eloped. Perhaps, *now*, Papa will devote some
of his attention to *her*. He could not get out of the
country fast enough when the scandal broke. Went off
to Crete to dig up his precious relics and no doubt
found comfort in moralising on the ephemeral nature
of human achievement."

"You are scathing," suggested her brother, not ill
pleased at the thought. "But his lordship must have
thought well of him to have left him this comfortable
holding."

Francesca bit her lip. "You are right," she admitted.
"And I should be ashamed to speak so, with no better
cause than childish annoyance. His lordship preferred
Mr. Develyn even to his heir. He said that the boy had
been unfortunate, having fallen in love with a pretty
face and a shallow mind before he was old enough to
know better." Her reluctant grin dawned. "A confirmed
bachelor himself, his lordship always knew just where
other men had erred in their choice. When he heard
of Mrs. Ramsey's death—for Mr. Develyn divorced
her, you know, so that she might marry her lover—
he expressed the hope that now his nephew might

marry again, using his judgement rather than his artistic tastes."

"Perhaps he will do so," said Geoffrey hopefully. "With such an establishment as Saxondene he will feel the need of a helpmeet to preside over his household and take charge of his daughter. And you will agree that it would be much more comfortable for *you* to have a pleasant neighbour."

"But who is to say that she would *be* pleasant?" laughed his sister. "Or even that she would deign to recognise my existence. No thank you. I do very well as I am. And *you* should be the first to admit I am well able to take care of myself," she added impishly, putting away the foils with which they had been engaged when the summons of the bell interrupted them. "Did I not give a good account of myself? And I am far more deadly with a pistol I promise you."

But though he laughed and acknowledged the verbal hit Geoffrey was not so easily distracted. "It's very fine talking," he protested, "but when I sail for India next month you will have no one of your own to take your part if you like your new landlord no better on closer acquaintance."

Francesca did not quite see how his support would be of use to her under those circumstances, but it would be unkind to say so. She said cheerfully, "Well if that is the case I shall pack my trunks and come running to my kind brother in India."

Since she was engaged in putting the case of foils back in its place she did not see the expression of almost ludicrous dismay that crossed her brother's ingenuous countenance at the playful suggestion. A week's close acquaintance with his rediscovered sister had taught him that she was quite capable of doing just that. Fran was a darling—well, no, she would not thank him for calling her that—she was—she was the best of good fellows. She was also, to say the least of it, unusual. And the thought of the impact that she would make on his colonel was enough to make a fellow break into a cold perspiration. Devoutly he prayed that amicable relations might be established between Saxondene and South Gates and resolved to take every opportunity of furthering this laudable end.

Three

"I think that answers most of my questions," said Mr. Develyn pleasantly. "I'll have to think about renewing Stoddart's lease but there's no hurry about that until next quarter day. Everything else seems quite straightforward. And I would like you to congratulate the servants on the excellent order in which they have maintained the place. Since all but Jessop are strangers to me it will come better from you. I was particularly pleased with the gardens, but that is probably because I had forgotten their charm and the variety that they offer. I would not overpraise the gardeners to the disappointment of those whose work has been just as faithfully done. But you will know just how and where to drop a word. There is just one small matter that still puzzles me. What has happened at the south lodge? And who is living there?"

The expression of gratification which had dawned on the steward's face at the words of commendation was wiped away. He straightened a little in his chair, ran a finger round his neckcloth as though, of a sudden, it felt tight, and cleared his throat quite unnecessarily. Though he then spoke with tolerable composure as though the enquiry was of no particular moment Mr. Develyn was aware of his hesitancy and realised that he had touched on a matter of some delicacy.

"South Gates, sir? His lordship and Miss Thornish chose the name when he had the house built for her, five years ago. It is Miss Thornish who resides there. And I believe at this present she has a brother staying with her."

It was an answer that posed a number of new questions. Who was Miss Thornish that his uncle should build a house for her within the bounds of his own park? Surely not one of his 'particulars'? His lordship's early career had become almost legendary for the number, distinction and charm of the highflyers whom he had taken under his protection from time to time, and in keeping with the tradition of his class he had treated them with open-handed generosity. But to be establishing one of them in a house on one of his own estates was a very different pair of shoes. Besides, now that he came to think about it, the wench was the wrong age. No more than twenty five, he reckoned. So she could scarcely be a relic of the Earl's romantic past, unless, indeed—the notion sudenly occurred to him— she was his natural daughter. *That* might fit. Despite the antagonism that she had aroused in him Mr. Develyn did Miss Thornish the justice of acknowledging that there was a look of breed about her. It would be as well to move carefully. He had no desire to be stirring up old scandals within a week of entering upon his heritage.

"Does Miss Thornish own the house or is she one of my tenants?" he asked, displaying only the mildest of interest.

"Well, sir, it is rather an awkward situation. The place was left to Miss Thornish for life, or until she marries. If she dies a spinster it reverts to the estate. If she marries, she forfeits the property but receives a handsome marriage portion in compensation. She pays no rent, so she can scarcely be described as a tenant, but during his lordship's lifetime it was customary for me to see to the proper maintenance of the property—minor repairs, you understand—and this practice I have continued. His lordship also set aside a portion of the stabling for the lady's use, saying that it was ridiculous to build more when there was already ample accommodation. During your absence abroad I felt that it was scarcely within my province to institute changes, but if you will acquaint me with your wishes I will inform Miss Thornish accordingly."

He seemed thankful to have finished his explanation. And small wonder, thought Mr. Develyn. What a damnable coil! He did not care to enquire more precisely but it seemed highly probable that the wretched female had been accustomed to having the freedom of the park and gardens. He would be forever running across her. And so far as he could see there was no hope of getting rid of her unless she married. And what man in his senses would take on such a termagant? Unless his uncle had endowed her with a portion so handsome as to persuade some suitor to overlook her outlandish ways.

He suggested that he and Shires should stroll down to the stables forthwith. He wanted to have a look at Rustic who was almost recovered from his mishap and Shires could show him which parts of the buildings had been at Miss Thornish's disposal. He wondered with some interest what sort of cattle she kept and whether she had her own groom and coachman or was accustomed to calling upon the services of the Saxondene staff. If, as he half expected, she was some kind of a cousin of his, he could scarcely begrudge her the privileges which his uncle had so casually bestowed. But it was going to be deuced awkward. They would have to come to some proper arrangement. Little as he relished the prospect he foresaw that it would shortly be his duty to pay a formal call upon the lady.

A suggestion to this effect was welcomed by his steward with such excessive enthusiasm that he was confirmed in his belief that the visit was likely to be an awkward one. He already knew that Miss Thornish was remarkably hot at hand. He had a strong suspicion that she would actually relish an encounter in which all the tactical advantages lay with her. Gloomily he helped Shires to sort and put away the formidable mass of documents relating to household expenses, tenancy agreements, tithe dues and wage bills that had been brought out for his inspection. Thanks to their exigencies the morning was far gone. He hoped Miss Thornish would not be inundated with afternoon callers. The presence of a brother, he felt, could only be helpful. A man was bound to take a more rational view of the difficulties of sharing entrance gates and stable accommodation. For a moment he speculated as to where a brother fitted into the pattern of Miss Thornish's background. Was he, perhaps, a half brother? Then, impatiently, he dismissed such idle conjecture. It was no bread and butter of his.

Mr. Shires, about to lock the massive desk, said suddenly, "I had almost forgot this, sir," and handed over a small sealed package. "The key to his lordship's strong-box," he explained. And since his new employer seemed faintly surprised, added, "You will find it in the bureau in your bedroom. His lordship used it mainly when travelling but I believe he always kept certain personal papers in it." He ventured a mild pleasantry. "The term strong-box is suggestive of hidden gold, is it not? But I fear you will be disappointed in that respect. Except for the necessities of travel his lordship was of the opinion that his gold was safer in the vaults of the bank." Mr. Develyn dropped the key into the capacious pocket of his riding coat. "In that case the treasure hunt may wait," he said, smiling. "Come and give me your opinion of my latest extravagance. Not that you will see him at his best, poor fellow, since he is still a little lame from my stupid mishandling on our journey here," and led the way out of the estate office into the golden September sunshine.

Strolling about the stables enabled him to forget for a while the minor irritation of having to come to terms with Miss Thornish. And the Earl had spoken truly when he had said that there was room and to spare. Even when he had purchased a couple of hacks, a pony for Robin and another hunter or two—if he could find anything of Rustic's stamp—it would still be true. He left Shires discussing the licensing of the several vehicles that stood in the vast coach house with Coates, the coachman, and went down the long rows of empty

stalls until he came to one which housed a good looking
brown gelding. One of Miss Thornish's he guessed,
just the right stamp of animal for a gig or a phaeton,
providing the driver knew what she was about. Investi-
gation in the coach house suggested that the lady drove
a fashionable dennet rather than the more commonplace vehicle of his imagining. He examined it with
interest, never having seen one at close quarters, and
was so engaged when the sound of hoofs and voices
caused him to turn. Miss Thronish rode into the yard
with a young gentleman in attendance.

Mr. Develyn bit back a hasty imprecation. Confound
the wench! Must she always take him at a disadvantage?
He knew that he must present all the appearance of one
prying into matters that were no concern of his. But
there was no help for it and explanation would only
give more importance to a trivial circumstance so he
came forward with the best grace that he could muster
to help the lady dismount.

He would scarcely have recognised her. Gone was the
insolent urchin who had outfaced him at his own
gates. In dark, close-fitting riding dress with sweeping
skirts, severe stock and hard hat she made him feel
shabby and unkempt, some humble peasant approaching a royal duchess. She accepted his help as though
it was only her due, although she thanked him prettily
enough and asked permission to present her brother
as though their earlier acquaintance had been on a
purely formal footing.

The three of them exchanged a few polite common-
places on the weather, the duration of Mr. Geoffrey
Thornish's stay and places of interest to be visited in
the vicinity. The conversational temperature rose a little

when Mr. Develyn was able to bestow sincere praise
on the horses that the pair had been riding. Miss Thornish told him that both were of the late Earl's breeding
and that she knew of no one to equal him as a judge
of horse flesh. She then enquired very civilly after
Rustic and admired the handsome pair that Mr. Develyn was accustomed to drive in his curricle. The courtesies having thus been duly observed, Mr. Develyn
enquired when it would be convenient for Miss Thornish to receive him as there were one or two matters he
would like to discuss with her. He thought she showed
a trace of wariness at this, but she assented equably
enough and it was arranged that he should call on her
that very afternoon. Then Mr. Shires rejoined the
party and after a little more desultory conversation the
Thornishes went off in the direction of South Gates
while Mr. Develyn and his steward continued their tour
of inspection.

Apprised in advance of the visit, Miss Thornish's
welcome *this* time was gracious formality itself. A smiling, chubby little maid servant ushered the visitor into
a room where brother and sister presented a charmingly domestic picture as they laughed and squabbled
over a cribbage board. It was a long room with an
unusually lofty ceiling and not in the least like any
lady's drawing room that he had ever seen before, its
size and severity relieved only by delicate plaster
mouldings and the fact that one wall consisted almost
entirely of windows which gave on to a pleasant ter-
raced lawn and an Italian garden. There were no pic-
tures, no ornaments, no feminine knick-knacks unless
one counted a curiously carved horse in what looked
to Mr. Develyn's collector's eye remarkably like green

jade which stood in a niche above the hearth. There
was not even very much furniture. One wall was lined
with books and there was a modern revolving book-
case beside the hearth. There were several comfortable
looking easy chairs, a pianoforte and a Pembroke table,
and that was about all. The room should have looked
austere, even bleak. Instead it was warm and welcoming. Walls and ceiling were tinted a soft yellow and
there were glowing pools of colour where one or two
carpets had been spread over the oak boards. Turkish,
those carpets, if his judgement was not in error, and
extremely costly, too. Their colours were repeated in
the window hangings and the damask coverings of
stools and cushions.

All this Mr. Develyn assimilated as he apologised
pleasantly for interrupting the game and accepted a
seat which proved to be just as comfortable as it looked.
Miss Thornish laughed and assured him that she, for
one, could only be thankful for the interruption, since
Geoffrey was possesed of the devil's own luck, and at
the present rate of progress she would soon find herself
without a feather to fly with. Mr. Develyn thought it a
pity that any lady should permit herself to use language
that smacked of Boodles or the Cocoa Tree. She was
quite a well-looking woman if you liked the proud
aquiline style. Indeed, his first impression as she rose
to greet him had been a pleasant one. He had thought
so tall a female well advised to dress so plain. Mr.
Develyn might be knowledgeable about oriental carpets but he was sadly ignorant about the niceties of
feminine dress. Miss Thornish's 'plain' gown came from
Paris and had cost perhaps three times as much as the

more elaborate creations to which his eye was accustomed.

Mr. Thornish opined with brotherly candour that Fran would never make a card player. "No idea at all of calculating the odds. Careless discards—reckless leads—no wonder you're at *point non plus*," he told her. "Do *you* care for cards, sir?"

Mr. Develyn admitted that in his younger days he had been partial to an occasion rubber of whist but had not played recently since card players were not exactly thick on the ground in the somewhat remote areas to which his recent travels had taken him.

"You'll find plenty of 'em here," said young Thornish cheerfully. "All kinds—though none of your true gamblers, of course. Seems to me it's about all there is to do in the winter on non-hunting days. You'll hunt, I suppose?"

"I shall hope to manage a day most weeks. I'm not a dedicated hunting man though I enjoy a good gallop as much as anyone else. Hunting three days a week is too hard on the horses unless you keep a far bigger stable than I can afford. Which is one of the things I wanted to discuss with you, Miss Thronish. I shall hope to buy one more hunter—possibly two, if I can find anything of the right stamp. Then there will have to be a pony for Robin—my daughter. Perhaps a couple of hacks. Will that leave sufficient accommodation for your horses? Are your hunters still out at grass?"

"I do not hunt, thank you. I have a young colt still out at grass, and he, with the two hacks you saw this morning and Chanterelle—the brown gelding—make up my stable."

He was a little surprised that she did not hunt. He

had seen enough this morning to suspect that she was a first rate horsewoman and had judged that the excitement, the display, even, perhaps, the risks of the hunting field would be very much to her taste. He said idly, with no real interest, "Then there will be ample accommodation for both of us. But how do you beguile the long winter days, Miss Thornish? As your brother says, there is not much else to do. And hunting does at least give one a good chance to meet one's neighbours."

"I wonder if the fox thinks so?" said Miss Thornish sweetly.

There was a brief startled silence. Mr. Develyn felt rather as though he had inadvertently plunged his hand into a wasps' nest. But he made a swift recover. "You must forgive my blunder," he said politely. "I was not aware that you had strong feelings on this subject. But, if I may steal your own phrase, I wonder how the hens feel when the fox pays them a midnight visit?"

"That is not at all the same," she retorted hotly. "The fox is only obeying his natural instincts—to kill, to eat, to provide for his mate and cubs."

"And when he goes through the chicken coop— killing and *not* eating? Killing for the sheer joy of it and leaving the headless corpses strewn on the ground to taunt their hapless owner? And she, perhaps, some poor widow body, bereft of her all?" The Irish lilt *would* creep in when he was amused.

Francesca did not reply. She knew that what he said was true—had seen similar evidence herself. But there was a defiant glint in her eye. She might, for the moment, be bested in argument, but she was not beaten.

"And if it's that wretched Reyna of yours that you're

thinking about, the sooner you get rid of her the better," put in Geoffrey briskly. "Mr. Develyn's in the right of it. You'll never tame the brute. Fran's quite besotted about animals, sir. This little beast was dug out of a burry last spring. An old dyke had flooded back and drowned the vixen and the rest of the litter, but this one came out alive. From what Coates tell me, m'sister tended the little beast with as much care as though it had been a thoroughbred hound pup. And got well bitten for her pains, more than once. Isn't that right, Fran?"

His sister gave a rueful grimace, the air of defiance fading. "True enough," she admitted, thoughtfully inspecting one slim hand which bore several white scar dimples. "No one could call Reyna tame. Nor is she an attractive pet, though she *is* very handsome," she added defensively. "But can you blame her for using her teeth? Her cosy familiar world had collapsed around her and she was determined to fight for her right to survive. For my part I applaud her attitude—even if I did not relish its manifestation," and she wrinkled an impudent nose at her brother.

Mr. Develyn could not help wondering what experience in Miss Thornish's past had induced this sympathetic attitude. "What will you do with her?" he asked curiously. "I believe it is almost impossible to domesticate a fox cub, yet you will hardly wish to keep her penned up for ever."

"I thought to release her next spring, keeping her safe through *this* hunting season at any rate," explained Miss Thornish rather crisply. "In that way she would have a reasonable chance of survival in natural conditions."

He nodded. "Yes. I expect that would be best. In that case perhaps you will permit me to bring Robin to see the creature. She would be interested, I am sure."

Miss Thornish agreed to the suggestion willingly enough and followed it up with several polite enquiries about his daughter. Geoffrey, who found these tepid exchanges boring, toyed idly with the playing cards and decided that Fran's new neighbour seemed pretty harmless. No one could call the fellow handsome, he thought comfortably, nor even modish. His dress was neat but too sober for Geoffrey's youthful notions, his crisp dark hair cut too short to be fashionable. His features were tolerably regular but his countenance lacked animation, the grey eyes coolly impersonal, the mouth harsh and unyielding, the lines about it bitter. An ill man to cross, concluded young Mr. Thornish, but not one to set a maiden heart in a flutter. And Fran seemed to have got over her initial annoyance with the fellow and was behaving very prettily, concealing the boredom that she, too, must be suffering. He awarded her an approving glance—and seeing that something had amused her paid more heed to the conversation.

"Poor woman! What a shocking cross for *any* female to bear—and worst of all for a governess! It is fortunate that she is employed to instruct one docile little girl and not a family of mischievous boys. Imagine what capital *they* would make of such a name! Turbot! Especially if she chanced to *be* fish-faced. Is she?"

"I believe the name is spelled T-E-R-B-E-R-T," explained Mr. Develyn solemnly. But his own lips twitched as he added, "*Not* like the fish. Nor is the lady fish-faced. Unless it be a shark," he finished thoughtfully, and smiled at Miss Thornish, a smile that so changed his whole appearance that it was fortunate that her brother chanced to be looking at *her*. "But it is very unkind in us to be speaking of her in this vein," he admonished. "I confess I did not take to her—thought her too severe and Robin *too* docile. But my mama-in-law assures me that she is most conscientious and extremely well qualified. It seemed to me—but there! I know nothing of bringing up a girl, not having been blessed with sisters. No doubt Lady Anley is the best judge."

He rose to take his leave, begging Miss Thornish to be sure to inform him if he could be of service to her in any neighbourly way. It was the merest formality. He had not the least expectation of being taken up on the offer and Francesca knew it. Afterwards she wondered what imp of mischief had prompted her to speak as she did. "I will certainly do so, sir," she told him, curtseying demurely. "Pray tell me, are you fond of fencing? Because I find myself sadly out of practice. Geoffrey will bear me out that I don't show too badly —for a female, of course"—this with a wicked glance at Geoffrey beneath lids modestly lowered—"and if you could spare the time to give me an occasional bout I might recover some degree of speed and precision."

It was Mr. Develyn's intention to refuse outright. Courteously, but quite definitely. He had never heard such an outrageous suggestion in all his life. Fence with a woman? Unthinkable! Unfortunately, before he could select just the words that would administer a polite but unmistakable set-down, Mr. Thornish intervened.

"Don't be beguiled by that miss-ish face, sir! Out of practice indeed! She was more than a match for me, and I had thought myself not wholly ignorant. Touched me wherever she chose. Says your uncle taught her himself, which would acocunt for it. But don't you let her make a fool of you!"

After that it was manifestly impossible to decline the invitation and keep his self respect. Mr. Develyn said, rather coldly, that he would be happy to afford Miss Thornish an opportunity to demonstrate her skill —a turn of phrase which the lady later described to her brother as horridly patronising—but that as he planned to travel up to Town on the following day to bring his daughter down to Saxondene, he feared that the engagement would have to be deferred. Restraining a tantalising impulse to suggest that he take one or two fencing lessons while he was in town, Miss Thornish bade him an equally chilly farewell.

Four

Mr. Develyn's journey was to no purpose. Upon arrival at Lord Anley's residence he found his daughter confined to her room with a feverish chill and quite unfit, pronounced Miss Terbert, to endure the rigours of a journey into Kent. Robin wept and pleaded. Mr. Develyn said that surely, if she was warmly wrapped, she would come to no harm, so mild and pleasant was the weather. But Lady Anley supported Miss Terbert's view of the case and Mr. Develyn was forced to bow to their superior knowledge of his daughter's constitution.

After kicking his heels restlessly in Town for several days he abandoned the attempt for the time being. But during those days the suspicion was gradually born in upon him that neither lady really looked with favour on the prospect of Robin's removal to Saxondene. That was a pity. He owed Lady Anley a debt of gratitude for the readiness with which she had undertaken the charge of her infant grand-daughter at so tender an age. She must always be a welcome visitor at Saxondene and he would be happy to lend Robin to her grandparents for frequent visits if they so desired. But Saxondene was now his home and his daughter's place was with him.

As for Miss Terbert he suspected that she was not anxious to quit the civilised comfort of the Metropolis for the isolation of rural Kent. So very cultured a female would undoubtedly prefer the amenities offered to the town dweller by the British Museum, the libraries and art galleries rather than the freedom to keep a pony and any number of pets which had so clearly enchanted his daughter.

These reflections he kept to himself, but in bidding good-bye to a very woe-begone Robin he found an opportunity to reassure her. He would come back—in two weeks' time at the very most—and carry her off willy-nilly. This should be a secret between them and not even Grandmama was to be admitted into it. He would just come, quite unheralded, and whisk her away to Saxondene. At which the miserable face brightened considerably and there was even a hint of excited colour in the pale cheeks. Then Miss Terbert came back into the room and he laid a conspiratorial finger across his lips before rising to say, "Be a good girl and take your medicine without fuss. Then, in a few weeks' time I will come again to see how you are doing."

Driving himself back to Kent—the mild autumnal weather still holding—he had ample opportunity for reflection. He was slightly annoyed by the delay, feeling that he had been fobbed off unnecessarily and that it was high time that he took Robin's upbringing into his own hands. Closer acquaintance had not increased his regard for Miss Terbert. He found her chill severity repellent. Lady Anley, on the other hand, was too inconsistent, neglecting to visit the schoolroom for days at a time, then indulging the child beyond reason when it chanced that no other engagement proved more attractive. Mr. Develyn was well aware that some of the blame for the failure of his marriage must be laid at his own door, but he could not help thinking that this sort of inconsistency had fostered just that volatility in his wife that he did not wish to see encouraged in his daughter. Some day, in addition to his very comfortable fortune, Robin would inherit Saxondene. He wanted her to grow up in the place and learn without realising it the duties and responsibilities that were as much a part of her inheritance as its privileges.

When he had spoken of coming for Robin in a few weeks' time, Miss Terbert had murmured something about taking her to the dentist before she left town and Lady Anley had bewailed the possibility of being bereft of her grandchild during the Christmas season —and Christmas still three months away! He began to consider the advisability of replacing Miss Terbert by a younger, more amiable female. One who was accustomed to country ways and would not fuss unduly over muddy shoes and torn petticoats. Not that one could dismiss the woman without due cause. But if one could find her an alternative post—one that would allow her to remain for most of the year in Town— he had no doubt that she would jump at the suggestion.

He did not, however, permit his preoccupation to lead him into error *this* time, taking good care to

approach his new home by its principal entrance. And
already it *was* home he realised, as he handed hat and
gloves to Jessop and shrugged himself out of his driving
coat. The old man was meticulously correct in enquiring as to the comfort of his journey and his re-
quirements in the way of refreshment but soon fell
into a more loquacious vein as he reported various
minor happenings which had occurred since Mr. Develyn's departure. There had been a message from Mr.
Gilbey at Fouracres inviting him to go over and look
at a promising five year old that should be well up to
his weight. An old elm had come down in Thursday's
high wind and damaged the hay barn at Rylands but
by good fortune no one was hurt. And young Mr.
Thornish had gone off to rejoin his regiment. There
was quite a pile of correspondence awaiting the master's attention and he would find it on the writing table
in the library.

He found Tara there, too, and was almost sub-
merged by her rapturous welcome. Like her master,
Tara had decided that Saxondene was home, and a
home far more appropriate to her noble breeding than
those she had known so intermittently in her nomadic
past. After due and dignified consideration of all its
offered amenities she had selected the library as her
special abiding place. Though *she* had no great love of
reading, her master had. She could spend blissful
hours sprawled across his feet, or, in moments of
greater animation, leaning heavily against his knees
and gently nudging his book until his hand moved
absently to caress her head and rub gently about the
base of her ears, an attention which induced in her a
mood of slant-eyed, drooling ecstasy.

Even lacking the heaven of her god's presence, the library had a good deal to recommend it. It was part of the original manor, a very ancient apartment facing north; so throughout the year one, at least, of its cavernous hearths was properly furnished with a glowing log fire. This warmed the surrounding stonework to a point at which a reasonable hound could afford to ignore the occasional draughts which really only served to underline the comfort in which she lay.

Having endured the first exuberance of greeting, Mr. Develyn eventually convinced his devoted attendant that he neither desired the extensive ablutions that she was eager to bestow upon him nor felt that a good long walk would be just the thing to set him up nicely after a forty mile drive. She accepted defeat and subsided with a heavy sigh beside his chair. He was surprised by the number of letters awaiting his attention after his brief absence. He had spent barely a month in the place and there had been little time for socialising. The pleasant sensation of home coming grew stronger. Not that there was anything out of the ordinary in the letters—just the day to day stuff of country living; an invitation to dinner from his nearest neighbours, the Staniforths of Easter Cote; a friendly note from Sir Lucas Godwin confirming that hounds would meet at Saxondene on the first Wednesday in November. There was also a letter from his brother, Edward, saying that it was high time that he paid them a long visit. He must bring Robin so that she might become better acquainted with her Develyn cousins. There was a pony that she could ride—one that the boys had outgrown—and since his two sons had no sister of their own a girl cousin would do them a deal of good. Only in the final paragraph did he strike a mildly reproachful note. Their father, he said, was in reasonably good health considering his age, but still lived very retired as he had done since their mother's death. It was difficult to persuade him to leave his own apartments if they had guests and the management of the estate now devolved wholly upon Edward. Since Edward was the elder son and heir, that was natural enough.

But though Papa had withdrawn from the activities of everyday life his mental faculties were alert as ever. Edward felt that he would value a visit from his second son. Robert must have wonderful travellers' tales to tell that would beguile the lonely hours for the old man. And it was three years since Lady Anley had last brought Robin to visit him. She was the only girl child of her generation and Papa had seen in her some resemblance to his much loved wife. In short it was Robert's filial duty to visit them as soon as he could conveniently do so.

Robert smiled. Edward was inclined to be pompous and his wife was such a pattern card for all the domestic virtues as to be a dead bore, but he valued their sterling qualities and held them both in affection. It was good to be wanted. He would certainly go home on a visit as soon as he had arranged his domestic affairs.

He ate his dinner in solitary state. Soon he would have Robin for company. She was quite old enough, he considered, to have her meals with him, save when he was entertaining. They had a good deal of lee-way to make up in getting to know one another. The thought that he would have to share her society with

Miss Terbert made him pull a wry mouth. Something would have to be done about *that*. Meanwhile he must see about a pony for the child. She had been carefully taught and showed both liking and aptitude for the equestrian art. And she had said to him, "Yes, Papa. I like it very well. But one cannot make a real friend of a hireling. Anyone who can pay the charges may ride Star. He's a nice fellow and I'm fond of him, but it's not the *same*. He's friends with everyone."

That was the first time that he had realised that Robin was growing up. It was the only time she had admitted him into her confidence. He had realised that she was becoming a person in her own right and that he scarcely knew her. He had not known his wife. He had been enchanted by her pretty face and beguiling ways and had foolishly assumed that her principles and tastes would match his own. When it was born in upon him that she had no higher interest in life than the latest modes and the most intriguing crim. cons., he had realised that he could no more make her happy than she could him. But by that time there had been Robin to think about. He had turned more and more towards his archaeological interests, keeping up a respectable façade of family life for the child's sake and leaving his wife to pursue her more frivolous amusements. Her subsequent elopement had shocked him deeply at the time but he now acknowledged that he had been a good deal to blame. Having married such a butterfly little creature he should have been at more pains to keep her content. At least he had given her the divorce that she had craved and he sincerely hoped that she had been happier with Adam Ramsey. But that did not excuse his own culpability. He would take more pains to understand his daughter.

The days slid past with a deceptive appearance of leisure. He was fully engrossed in drawing the reins of the estate into his own hands. Coming virtually as a stranger, not knowing the place or its people, it was exacting work demanding both tact and patience to establish the sound understanding that was essential for harmony. Because the pace of his dealing was necessarily slow he could scarcely believe that close upon two weeks had elapsed since he had left Town and that it was time he went off to rescue Robin.

A letter from Lady Anley brought his promise to mind and for this he was duly grateful though the letter itself annoyed him considerably. The dear child was much better, his mama-in-law assured him, well enough to resume her studies though still sadly pulled down. It would be most imprudent, at this stage, to remove her from the care of the family physician who was well acquainted with her constitutional delicacy and who could be summoned at once if she suffered any set-back.

Constitutional fiddlestick thought Mr. Develyn, his brows knitting in the black scowl that had caused a long-ago tutor with a taste for Plantagenet history to address him playfully as Robert the Devil. The women were determined to keep Robin from him. He would have to cut through the web of half-hints and re-proaches in which they were trying to tangle him and carry her off forthwith. If he travelled up to Town tomorrow evening and stayed the night at a hotel, he could descend upon Anley House unheralded next day and see for himself how matters stood. If *he* decided that Robin was well enough to travel—in a luxurious carriage, with hot bricks and fur rugs to guard against any possibility of chill—then travel she should, even if he took her in the clothes she stood up in. There was bound to be a fuss about packing for her and that would mean further delay while her jealous guardians sought about for other excuses to detain her.

He sought out his housekeeper and asked her to see that the rooms set aside for Miss Terbert and his daughter were made ready for occupation. The good lady bridled offendedly at the request.

"The rooms have been kept in readiness, sir, since first you gave orders. I saw to it myself, *and* the airing of the beds, seeing as Miss Robin had been poorly and not being one that cares to be neglectful of such matters."

He realised that he had offended and hastened to make amends. "*That* I know very well, Mrs. Johnson. If I did not, I have but to look about me." His gesture indicated such genuine appreciation of the well kept room that she unbent a trifle, and when he went on, smiling, "You stand in more danger of a scolding for doing too much. When I consider all the work that has been put upon you by my homecoming, and no extra staff engaged as yet, I really do not know how you have contrived so well."

At this Mrs. Johnson beamed upon him, her ruffled feathers smoothly composed once more, and said, "About the extra staff, sir. You did say I was to make enquiries in the village, and with Miss Robin and her governess coming we could do with another girl to wait on the schoolroom. Miss Thornish says we couldn't do better than take on Becky Marlow."

"Miss *Thornish* says?" The surprise in his voice was

audible, even to an insensitive ear. Had the Rector's wife, or, indeed, any of the married ladies of the neighbourhood been quoted as the authority, he would not have thought to question it. But why Miss Thornish?

Mrs. Johnson was unperturbed. "Yes, sir," she said confidently. "Very good with the girls, is Miss Thornish. Has them up to her house of an evening and teaches them all sorts of things. A bit of reading and writing for those that have a fancy for it, but mostly fine sewing and how to get up lace and linen nicely and to dress meat and such. As well as speaking in a proper fashion, which I must say is a good thing, for with some of them straight from home you can't understand one word in ten."

Mr. Develyn blinked. This picture of a maiden lady given to good works sorted ill with his own mental image of an impudent hoyden who had first snubbed him at his own gates and then called his swordsmanship in question. *That* challenge had slipped his memory, absorbed as he had been in matters of more import. It would have to wait, now, until he had Robin safely installed at Saxondene.

"You will do just as you think best, Mrs. Johnson," he said. "I have complete confidence in your judgement, as you appear to have in Miss Thornish's."

He sat late that night, catching up on neglected correspondence, and perhaps as a consequence, slept badly. That was a new come-out. For years he had been the lightest of sleepers. When life and liberty had frequently depended upon the ability to rouse to instant alertness at the slightest sound, it had been essential. But since coming into Kent he had recaptured the happy knack of falling instantly into sound sleep as soon as he had put out his candle. Tonight sleep evaded him, his mind busily reviewing the tasks that might be accomplished in the morning and those that had best be deferred until his return. Presently the personality of Miss Francesca Thornish obtruded itself into his thoughts. Odd creature! Who would have expected her to concern herself with the welfare of servant girls? He must certainly cross foils with her—literally, he smiled to himself in the darkness, and probably in the metaphorical sense too, if past experience was any guide! It was years since he had indulged in sword play but he had little doubt of being able to give a good account of himself. Certainly too good for any female to be able to best him. He wondered what trick she had used to discomfit her brother, and drifted at last into uneasy slumber. Since he could not endure to sleep with drawn curtains, first light awakened him. Awakened him to a mood of restless energy to which, of late, he had been a stranger. He could not lie idling a-bed with so much to be done before he set out for Town, even though he was perfectly well aware that there was very little he could usefully achieve until the rest of the world aroused itself from slumber.

Subdued sounds indicated that the servants at least were astir, though it was improbable that his valet was one of them! Fortunately he was still capable of dressing himself without assistance—indeed, preferred to do so—though it was very comfortable to have his gear kept in good order without effort on his part. He had never been a dressy man but he did like fresh linen, perhaps in reaction against the years when his shirts had so often been full of sand or strange insects; had so often clung to his body with the sweat of his labours.

He washed in cold water from the ewer—no need to trouble the servants for hot water at this hour—shaved rather sketchily and dressed in shabbily comfortable riding clothes. There was Tom Gilbey's bay in his stables. Tom had suggested that he try the beast for a week or two before deciding whether to buy him. He had agreed. The bay's performance was impressive, his speed quite startling. He was still a bit raw, a trifle headstrong, but given time to mature and firmly handled he might some day be almost as good as Rustic. Gilbey was asking a stiff price for him but he was worth it. He would exercise Hopover—for such was the unfortunate animal's name—and see how he behaved in the chill of early morning when so many horses were inclined to sulk.

There were still faint swirls of mist in the valley bottom and the grass was rimed with frost where the sun had not penetrated. Autumn was come in earnest, though the long dry spell still held. Hopover disliked the steady jog on which his rider insisted. Mr. Develyn explained to him soothingly that this was the stuff to build muscle and that he should have a chance to shake the fidgets out of his feet presently. The intelligent ears flickered attentively to the sound of the deep slow voice but still he pulled and still Robert was aware of the vibrant energy between his knees, the leashed power that was only waiting upon opportunity. Hopover needed riding. There was no malice in him but no one was ever going to describe him as a safe easy ride.

Early as it was they were not the only ones abroad. Once they checked—to Hopover's dancing resentment —while a flock of sheep surged past them. And two fields away a boy was exercising a young horse. The animal took Mr. Develyn's eye immediately. Young as he was there was high breeding manifest in every line of the rangy black body. He wondered who the horse belonged to—and if the owner even knew that it was being ridden, for the boy was riding without a saddle and the two of them were larking about in what Mr. Develyn considered a foolishly reckless fashion though even at that distance it was possible to sense the sympathy between them.

On impulse he put Hopover at the first of the low hedges that separated him from the frolicking pair. True to his name the delighted animal cleared it easily and cantered gaily towards the second obstacle. The sudden appearance of another horse and rider seemed to startle the black colt for he broke into a headlong gallop, racing towards the distant wall that bordered the turnpike. Horrified, believing the colt to be bolting and out of control, Mr. Develyn launched Hopover in pursuit, praying that the horse's speed would enable him to ride off the black before he crashed—as inevitably he must—at the wall.

But even with spurs driven home, Hopover could not reduce the black colt's lead. They were doing more harm than good, for the sound of hoofs pounding behind would certainly do nothing to deter the runaway. Mr. Develyn slackened speed and waited, grim-faced, for the fall that must ensue.

Almost at once the black colt's speed eased. Thankfully, if disbelievingly, Mr. Develyn watched him come round in a wide right-hand circle and canter back towards Hopover, his feelings divided between an annoyance that stemmed largely from relief and a whole-hearted appreciation of the colt's beautiful action and faultless conformation. What a magnificent creature he would be when he was fully furnished! He reined in, the better to study that perfection, watching the canter change to a trot and then to a collected walk, the rider obviously delighting in displaying his mount's performance.

Only at the last moment, as the black drew to a halt beside Hopover, did Mr. Develyn spare any attention for the boy on his back. And then his gaze widened into blazing indignation. For the face beneath the soft peaked cap was the face of Francesca Thornish and she was plainly in a high gig, the golden eyes alight with teasing laughter, pleasure and triumph bubbling from her lips.

"Wasn't he marvellous? I've been longing to try him against Hopover. He's supposed to be the fastest in these parts, you know. But Merlin has the heels of him —you saw for yourself—and I wasn't even pressing him!"

In her eagerness, with parted lips and the faint flush of exertion in her cheeks, she was a bewitching sight. The boy's cap she wore was tilted at a rakish angle, her shirt open to reveal a beautifully rounded throat, and she seemed quite unconscious that there was anything out of the way in her workmanlike ride-astride attire. Even Mr. Develyn, despite deep annoyance that he had permitted himself to feel a considerable degree of anxiety for this impenitent brat, was not unconscious of her attraction. Despite the masculine attire he saw her for the first time as a woman—warm, glowing, vital. And a rare handful she would be, he told himself severely, clutching at the remnants of common sense.

Neither to hold nor bind, and with no notion at all of the behaviour proper to a lady.

He pulled himself together. "Your horse is a magnificent creature," he said repressively. "But do you not think he is too strong for a lady? Stallions—even young ones—are unpredictable. To speak the truth I thought he had got away with you just now."

Her expression hardened. The impulsive confiding girl was gone. "Were you hurrying to my rescue? How chivalrous! But quite unnecessary. Merlin and I understand each other very well. It is not in his nature to serve me a dirty trick just because he is stronger than I. He is—I was about to say—a gentleman. But that is scarcely to do him justice."

The wretched girl had a knack of twisting everything a man said to put him out of countenance. To be sure he had no right to question her actions. If she chose to break her neck it was quite her own affair. And since she so plainly preferred the horse's society to his, he would leave her to enjoy it. He apologised coldly for his unwarrantable presumption and wheeled Hopover about.

"Now you are angry with me," he heard her say, "and with good cause. I should not have ripped up at you like that, for you have shown me nothing but courtesy. The trouble is that in my dealings with your uncle I never learned to keep my tongue. To him he would always have me speak what was in my mind. *From* him I caught the trick of depressing pretension with a cutting phrase. It amused him to hear me do it and I would sometimes exercise my wits just to make him smile. So I say sharp things and do not always mean them. And then, you see, he never—never—

cossetted me is the word, I think. I must make my own foolish mistakes, he said, and learn from them. And at first I made a great many," she remembered, her sober expression yielding to a rueful twinkle. "I think I may safely say that nowadays I know my own limitations— at least where horses are concerned. That's not to say I don't still take the occasional tumble," she added hastily, as though fearing to be thought boastful.

The cold anger in Mr. Develyn's eyes had melted. He had turned at her first words and studied her curiously as she made her awkward apology. She was not very good at it, he thought amusedly, and was the more inclined to credit her sincerity.

"The best of us do that," he said pleasantly. "As for a heedless dolt who puts a good horse at a jump without a thought for what may lie beyond it, so that the poor beast goes lame for a sennight, *he* should be sunk beneath reproach. Certainly he is the last man who should venture to advise others."

She was quick to catch the reference. Here were manners and a generosity that she understood and liked. She turned towards him eagerly and put out her hand—a spontaneous, boyish gesture as natural as breathing. "Friends?" she said childishly, slender dark brows quizzically raised.

Mr. Develyn grinned as he clasped the cool fingers firmly in his own. "Friends, of course," he assured her. And then broke into gentle laughter. "Until we cross swords!" he reminded her.

Five

This time Mr. Develyn took precautions to ensure that his journey should not be wasted. He travelled up to Town in his own chaise and even took the trouble to order the necessary changes of horses for his return so that there could be no question of delay. Descending upon Anley House in the middle of the morning, he found his mama-in-law still in her dressing room and his daughter at her lessons in the schoolroom.

Books and pen went flying as Robin sprang up and ran to hug him—a piece of spontaneity that earned her a reproof from Miss Terbert for such hoydenish behaviour. Mr. Develyn, one arm round the child's slim shoulders, begged pardon for disturbing the morning's studies and announced his intention of carrying his daughter off to take luncheon with him before setting out for Saxondene. He felt the child's body stiffen and saw the trouble in her face. With a reassuring squeeze of her shoulders he said cheerfully, "Away with you and put on your bonnet and cloak. And don't dawdle. I've ordered the chaise for a half after noon."

She fled—thankfully, he was sure, and he turned to confront Miss Terbert who had drawn herself up to her full height and appeared to be swelling visibly in the effort to control her anger.

"Pray do not be thinking that I wish *you* to put yourself about, ma'am," he said pleasantly. "A few days' holiday will do my daughter no harm and will give you leisure to make your own arrangements in comfort. If you will just see that the child has her night-rail and enough clothes for a day or two, the rest of her gear can come down by carrier and I will send my chaise for you in—shall we say a week's time?"

But Miss Terbert had no use for conciliatory approaches. "May I ask if Lady Anley is aware of this arrangement?" she enquired in arctic tones.

"Not yet," returned Mr. Develyn affably. "I am just about to inform her. But as I am told that she is dressing for a luncheon engagement I mustn't detain her too long. So if you will just arrange for Robin's bag to be packed?" And he bowed and left her.

It was not to be supposed that he could carry the matter so high-handedly without further opposition. Robin's packing was delegated to one of the maids— despite Mr. Develyn's pleasant manner, Miss Terbert did not quite dare to ignore his expressed request— and the lady herself came, uninvited, to join the debate in Lady Anley's dressing room. *Quite* above herself, concluded Mr. Develyn, and blamed Lady Anley's lazy amiability for permitting this domineering female to behave as though she ruled the roost. Prior to her intrusion he had fended off both argument and plea with kindly patience, even promising to ensure that Robin did not fall into idle ways because of an unexpected holiday. He, himself, would attend to her progress in the liberal arts, a high-sounding phrase which impressed Lady Anley and was capable, decided its inventor, of a liberal interpretation. He frankly admitted that he could not be of much assistance with such necessary social accomplishments as water colour sketching or music, but surely the loss of a week's practice would not be fatal?

"Miss Terbert assures me that Robin has considerable musical talent," said Lady Anley pensively. "I cannot imagine why! Her Mama could not so much as sing a hymn in tune. And you? No. I thought not. But so it is. And one must not inhibit genius, you know," she ended hopefully.

"Talent is scarcely genius, ma'am. And in any case, a week's deprivation will only stimulate her interest. As for your missing the child, this I understand. It grieves me that you should have such beggar's thanks after all that you have done for her. I can only repeat that you will always be a most welcome guest at Saxondene, and that Robin may visit you as often as you choose to invite her. For the rest—you are a great gardener, ma'am. You know far better than I that a young plant must be moved to its proper place before it becomes too well established in the nursery bed. Since Robin's future must lie at Saxondene, the sooner she accustoms herself to her new home, the better."

The compliment to her floricultural skill—one that she could honestly accept—proved a clincher as far as Lady Anley was concerned. She nodded agreement with her son-in-law's view, and, having done so, could scarcely refuse her consent to this present rather hasty departure. But, she ventured dubiously, glancing at the governess's disapproving face, "I do not know if Miss Terbert will be agreeable to taking up residence in Kent."

At this juncture Miss Terbert decided that the time had come to play her trump card. "I am not averse to spending a part of the year in rural surroundings," she informed them kindly. "But I could never consent to reside there permanently. However, I have received a very flattering offer from Lady Thomason who has been pressing me for some time to undertake the instruction of her children. A little out of hand, I fear, their dear Mama being so much taken up with her literary pursuits, but *that* I should soon remedy. So far I have refused to desert my post," she continued nobly, "but if Mr. Develyn adheres to his present plans I shall feel myself at liberty to yield to Lady Thomason's persuasions."

Not by the flicker of an eyelash did Mr. Develyn betray his delight. His expression was gravely sympathetic as he said, "You should do so at once, my dear ma'am. I quite understand that life in the country would be intellectual exile to a lady of your attainments. You must not even consider it. And *I* shall not permit your loyalty, your conscientious scruples to prevent you from accepting so advantageous an offer. *Four* children, I believe? Think of the scope for your abilities! You should write to Lady Thomason without delay."

Miss Terbert could not see quite how she had been manœuvred into a position from which it was impossible to withdraw. She had not the least desire to exchange her comfortable post at Anley House for a far more onerous one with a lady whose literary pretensions served largely as an excuse for an ill-run household and obstreperous children. But Mr. Develyn had left her no way out. And since she was not without her pride she did not whine. She curtsied politely and said that she would certainly take his advice, but could not resist adding that she hoped he would not have cause to regret his hasty decision.

Since Lady Anley was already protesting that she would be quite shockingly late for her party, Mr. Develyn was allowed to bear his daughter off without further delay. Her ladyship was less concerned with the parting itself than with her fear that Robin's farewell hug and kiss might disarrange the charming arcade—a confection of lace, parma violets and silver ribbons—which her maid had just set tenderly upon her elaborate coiffeur. Miss Terbert shook hands with her pupil and dourly expressed the hope that she would not allow herself to be diverted from the habits of regular study in which she had been so carefully trained, and father and daughter made good their escape, though it was not until they stopped for the first change of horses with London really left behind that Robin heaved a huge sigh, slipped a confiding little hand into her father's strong one, and said, "I can't really believe it yet, Papa. It's too good to be true. That I'm really going to live with you and Tara always. And better still—no Fish!"

She saw her father's startled expression, choked on a suppressed giggle and explained, "I always called her that, you know, to myself."

But on careful casual enquiry it emerged that the
governess had not been actively unkind. Robin's life
had been dull, lacking in warmth and laughter, but
not unhappy. There had been a great deal of work and
very little play because none of the people in Grandmama's circle had children of Robin's age. Between
Grandmama and Miss Terbert the little girl had learned
to melt into her background and speak only when she
was spoken to—a timid, decorous shadow of a child.
He fell silent awhile, wondering how he could contrive
young companionship for her. He would be in no hurry
to engage a new governess. To neglect her books for
a while would do little harm. There was plenty to be
learned, walking and riding about the place with him.

Beside him Robin sat quiet as a mouse. She was
bubbling with excitement and longing to ask a dozen
different questions but dared not venture them until
Papa seemed disposed to talk again. Stealing a sidelong
glance at him she thought he looked rather grim. Perhaps he was like Miss Terbert and did not care for
travelling in carriages. Presently she began to feel a
trifle queasy herself. Papa had given her a delicious
luncheon with all the things that she liked best to eat,
but between excitement and the swaying of the chaise
it was, perhaps, a pity that she had partaken of them
so freely. She was very thankful indeed when they
stopped to change horses for the last time. This time
Papa would not permit her to climb down and watch
the operation, lest she should take cold from the evening air. Nor, in the growing dusk, did he notice the
tiny shudder that she could not wholly repress as
she politely declined his suggestion of a glass of milk.
They set off again, Mr. Develyn announcing cheerfully

that now they would soon be home and a little disappointed that his daughter showed no animation at the prospect, Robin with lips pressed together and clammy little hands tightly gripped in her lap, silently praying that she might endure to the end.

Alas! The last stretch of the road was particularly trying, twisting to left and right in swift succession. It was too much for her. Just as Papa said, "See the lights, Robin? That is the south gate. We shall be home in ten minutes," a pitiful little wail fell on his ears.

"Ask him to stop, Papa! Quickly! I feel sick. And"—with a pathetic attempt at gallantry that made him ache with tenderness—"I mustn't be sick in your beautiful chaise, must I?"

If he had had any sense at all, Mr. Develyn told himself bitterly, or more experience with children, he might have guessed the cause of that long silence. He flung open the door of the chaise and let down the steps, sprang down himself and lifted Robin out. She stumbled to the hedgerow, clinging to his arm and was promptly very sick indeed. With one arm about her waist and the other hand supporting her forehead, Mr. Develyn acquitted himself quite adequately, memories of his own childish sufferings coming to his aid. When the first paroxysm abated he pulled out a handkerchief and mopped her up as best he could in the flickering light of the carriage lamp. She was struggling with tears and said, on a gulp, "I'm s-sorry, Papa. I tried very hard not to be sick but I c-couldn't h-help it," and was sick again.

This second spasm left her so limp and exhausted that he thought she was going to faint. Fortunately help was at hand if in rather quaint guise. Two sturdy little maidens came trotting hand in hand down the south drive, stopped immediately at the sight of Mr. Develyn's dilemma and came to enquire if they could be of any assistance. By the light of the lantern that they carried he recognised one as Miss Thornish's young maid.

"My daughter," he explained briefly. "She is carriage sick. Could you bring me a glass of cold water?"

"Yes, sir. And I'll ask Mrs. Hornby for the loan of her smelling salts as well," offered the damsel obligingly. "Do you wait here for me, Becky. I'll not be long." And taking the lantern from her friend's hand she hurried back towards South Gates.

Upon her return, however, she brought neither water nor smelling salts. And the tall, slender figure of her companion, even though muffled in a cloak against the evening chill, was certainly not the rotund and placid Mrs. Hornby. Miss Thornish herself had come to offer hospitality.

"Pray bring her indoors at once, sir," she begged. "She will take a chill if you linger here. I have all the restoratives a child could possibly require, but if it is travel sickness, as Marian tells me, then rest and warmth are all she really needs."

Mr. Develyn hesitated only briefly, then gathered Robin in his arms and followed his hostess, murmuring thanks and apologies for disturbing her. "This business of arriving on your doorstep in urgent need of assistance seems to be becoming a habit with me," he said ruefully. "Moreover, once again it is quite my own fault. I should have seen how it was with the poor child and insisted that she rest when we changed horses. But no, I could think only of pushing on as swiftly as possible."

"Gentlemen do not usually notice such things," Miss Thornish told him kindly. "And I am very sure that your daughter did her best to hide her discomfort from you. Then it would grow rapidly worse with the darkening, you know, until it was too great to be borne. At least it was always so with me, when I was a child. There! Put her in this chair, sir, propped up with cushions—so—and her feet on this stool. Marian, go bring a shawl to tuck round her, and Becky, do you take off her shoes and rub her feet, for I'll wager they're cold as ice. Gently, child! 'Tis not a floor you are polishing!"

She turned back to Mr. Develyn who was regarding his daughter's closed eyes and sickly pallor with some concern. "She will be better directly," she reassured him. "I expect she still feels the sway of the carriage. It is a horrid feeling but it soon passes. Just let her rest quietly for a while. May I offer you some refreshment after your journey? A glass of wine, perhaps?" She grinned suddenly, the mischievous gamin grin that seemed so much more characteristic of her than the sympathetic glance she had bestowed upon Robin. "It is quite safe, I promise you. Your uncle stocked my cellars himself. The Marsala, I believe, is perfectly acceptable to a discriminating palate."

Mr. Develyn thanked her but declined, saying that he had best instruct the post-boy to take the chaise on up to the coach house. It was already growing late and the lad would have to take the horses back.

"I can carry Robin if she is not able to walk," he explained.

"Will you not rather leave her with me for the night?" suggested Miss Thornish. "Her bed is what she really needs, poor lamb, and it would be a pity to cloud her home coming by carrying her up the drive in the darkness when she can see nothing of the gardens and, indeed, can scarcely hold up her head or keep her eyes open. Leave her with me tonight and by morning she will be restored to herself and able to savour everything to the full."

"But it is to take advantage of your kindness," protested Mr. Develyn. "No doubt you have engagements——" He allowed the sentence to trail off. It was so much the best, the most sensible plan—if she really meant it.

"No engagements and no advantage taken," said Miss Thornish firmly. "She may have Geoffrey's room. The bed is well aired and freshly made up, and Becky, here, shall tend her. Your mother will not mind, Becky, if we send a message. Becky is to be your daughter's maid," she added in an explanatory aside, "it will be a good beginning in her new duties."

Mr. Develyn nodded understanding. "Then we will consult Robin's wishes," said Miss Thornish, and went to kneel beside the small crumpled creature in the big chair.

"Will you stay here tonight, my dear? You shall go straight to your bed, with, perhaps a tisane of raspberry leaves—for that is a great specific against any kind of sickness—and perhaps a dry biscuit to nibble, if you should care for it." The beautiful voice dropped to an almost crooning note. "There will be no noise and no fuss. Just a warm cosy bed and quietness. And in the morning you will wake up perfectly well again, to enter into your new kingdom. Will you stay with me?"

Through the daze of nausea Robin had heard that voice saying various comfortable sensible things. Had even summoned energy to wonder how its owner knew that darkness made the sick feeling worse. Because it *did*. Now that same voice seemed to lay a soothing spell upon her present miseries, not the least of which was the fear of disappointing Papa. She opened heavy-lidded eyes languidly and looked up at her hostess.

The eyes that met hers were very clear, warm and gentle, though the lady's face was clean-cut, almost hard. The eyes and the voice went together, thought Robin hazily, but the face was somehow at variance. Yet instinctively, immediately, she trusted their owner.

"Yes please, ma'am, if Papa is willing," she said shyly.

"And you would like Papa to carry you up to bed as soon as he has seen to the horses?" went on the persuasive voice. "Good. Ask Mrs. Hornby for a hot brick, Marian. Her feet are still very cold. Becky, do you go with Mr. Develyn. He will give you Miss Robin's night bag."

Mr. Develyn found himself moving in docile obedience to these instructions—handing over Robin's portmanteau, settling up with the post-boy and then returning to Miss Thornish's drawing room to carry his daughter upstairs to a pleasant bed-chamber where a newly lit fire was crackling a welcome and Becky was hanging Robin's nightgown to warm in front of it.

With a promise that she would come back very soon with the tisane that she had suggested and see her guest comfortably settled for the night, Miss Thornish escorted Mr. Develyn downstairs once more and bade him goodnight, checking his attempts at expressing his gratitude with one of her mischievous chuckles and a brisk, "Pooh! So much ado for so small a service! If you *will* have the truth, sir, I'm delighted to have the chance of putting you under an obligation! I have the feeling that it may come in very useful!"

Mr. Develyn laughed, said that he would bear that in mind the next time he felt like picking a quarrel with her, and strolled home, his mind at rest as regards his daughter and thus free to ponder the new facets of Miss Thornish's personality that had been revealed to him tonight. On the whole, he thought, he liked her. Certainly he admired her competence. And if her manners and speech were boyishly careless and her liking for masculine dress still seemed to him wholly reprehensible, it was at least a change from the simpering posturings of fashionable beauties. Tonight, in her handling of Robin, he had caught a glimpse of the femininity that she was at such pains to hide. And it had seemed to him a comfortable and pleasant aspect of her nature, the more so that she did not flaunt it. Then Tara's ecstatic welcome drove thoughts of any other female from his mind and he settled down to his belated dinner.

But he was not yet quite done with Miss Thornish. When he retired to bed his valet drew his attention to a small sealed package lying on the dressing table.

"During your absence today, sir, I took the opportunity to press some of your coats. This was in the pocket of your *old* riding coat," he explained, with delicate emphasis on the adjective. Mr. Develyn grinned. Jenkins had already tried to persuade him that so ancient and shabby a garment was quite unbecoming to the dignity of the master of Saxondene. He picked up the package and recognised it as the one which Shires had given him—why—a month and more since! The key to the strong-box. Since he had chosen to occupy a room that faced north to the stone hills in preference to the larger apartment that the Earl had always used, the presence of the strong-box in the walnut bureau had quite gone out of his mind. He would go and investigate its contents at once.

He allowed Jenkins to help him into a dressing gown that fully satisfied the valet's sartorial standards, since it was as luxurious as the riding coat was shabby, then dismissed the man, picked up one of the candles from his dressing table, and strode off down the corridor to the Earl's room. Save for the strong-box the bureau was empty. And when he opened the box—a heavy, iron-hooped coffer of some antiquity—it, too, was almost empty. It contained only one item—a letter addressed to himself in his uncle's hand.

It was chilly in this unoccupied room. Mr. Develyn thrust the letter into his dressing gown pocket, locked the empty coffer and returned to the comfort of his bedroom fire.

To be reading a letter from a man who had been a twelve month in his grave induced in him a strange, solemn feeling. He did not even care to break the Earl's seal, sliding his pocket knife carefully beneath it so that it was undamaged. But this sober mood was not destined to last long. The letter covered four pages in the Earl's sprawling hand and its tone was nicely

calculated to dispel gloomy thoughts. It began without
preamble.

So you've survived to inherit. Surprising! Nevertheless, my felicitations. Having kept an avuncular
eye on your career as time and opportunity served,
I half expected you to pre-decease me. That would
have put me to some inconvenience—you've no idea
what a business the lawyers make of a simple matter
like changing one's Will. Permit me to express my
thanks to you for having the decency to outlast me
and to acknowledge that there were times when it
seemed doubtful. Henry Salt told me of your goings
on in Gizeh with Belzoni, but what the devil were
you up to in Crete? That's a tale I'd have liked to
hear—and one time I began to think I'd need to
seek a new master for Saxondene!

And now you're wondering what maggot got into
my brain to cause me to leave it to you. There were
two reasons. First—I didn't want Wilfred to have it.
No need for you to feel guilty about *that*. With all
the Irish estates and the industrial property in the
north—which pays a damned sight better than the
agricultural holdings—Wilfred has more than
enough. More, I daresay, than he can handle. I
wanted Saxondene well cared for and I think you
are the man to do it. You've outgrown the follies of
youth—or you should have done—and you're of an
age to know that there's nothing in this world so
satisfying as land. Good, solid land; and animals, and
simple people. Treat 'em right—and they'll do right
by you. There's nothing to equal the sight of your
own acres bearing good sound crops; your own

cattle fattening on pastures that your careful husbandry has enriched. And the folk who will work with you honestly and faithfully, serving the land as you do, are the salt of the earth and deserve well of you. I look to you, nephew, to see that they get their due.

Saxondene won't make you a wealthy man—but you've money enough and won't care for *that*. What it can give you is a home and work that is worth doing. It *could* also keep you from dying of dysentery as poor Belzoni did—or stifling to death in a heap of crumbling mummy dust. Pah! What a repulsive thought!

So take it, with my affection and good will, dear boy. I always liked you the best of my brood of nephews. There's a touch of the old Plantagenet devil in you still. I fear there was more than a touch in me. I wonder if there's any truth in that pretty legend that embroiders our family tree? Perhaps when I am summoned to join the shades of our ancestors I shall find out. Your worthy brother Edward I found a dead bore. Prudish, too, which in a man I hold unpardonable. As for Wilfred and Bryan —but you will form your own judgements.

Finally I would commend to your care one Francesca Thornish. To save idle conjecture let me say at once that the lady was never my mistress, nor is she my natural daughter. And since I shall be dead and gone when you read this I will freely confess that she is the only woman who ever had the opportunity of refusing me in marriage. I leave that fact as it stands. As I said apropos your cousins, you will judge for yourself. There are occasions when a woman, however intelligent and courageous, may be grateful for masculine support. If ever you can be of service to Francesca, serve her for my sake. I stand deeply indebted to her for the companionship, the amusement and—I think I may say —the affection that she has given me. I know my Francesca. She will never appeal for your help however deep her trouble—will probably resent it if offered. But if you can keep a protective eye upon her without her becoming aware of it, you will oblige.

Your dissolute and wholy unrepentant uncle,

FINMORE.

Mr. Develyn read this lengthy missive twice. It gave much food for thought. Lord Finmore had spoken of two reasons for his bequest, yet had only explained one. Was the unofficial guardianship of Francesca Thornish the second reason? Surely not! The Earl must have known that the task was virtually impossible. How *could* he guide and support a lady of decided views who was no relation of his? Naturally he would do whatever he could, as much, now, in gratitude for Robin's sake as for his uncle's asking. But beyond the trivial courtesies that were proper under the circumstances he was not prepared to go. He could offer the use of his chaise to drive into Tunbridge Wells—the freedom of the library—she was probably accustomed to that any way. He could put the resources of the gardens, succession houses and home farm at her disposal. But 'deep trouble' was a very different matter and Mr. Develyn shied away from it like a frightened horse.

Eventually he managed to conjure up one or two highly improbable circumstances in which his assistance might be of use to the lady without causing embarrassment to himself. The dismissal of an insolent manservant perhaps; or help with travelling arrangements if she wished to go abroad. An inner voice suggested that she was just as capable as he of dealing with such matters. But perhaps his uncle, a much older man, had not thought so. Perhaps that was the kind of thing he had meant. At least he allowed this comfortable notion to lull him to sleep.

Six

"I see that you favour the Italian school," commented Mr. Develyn, examining a pair of foils.

"Milord was tutored in the Italian style," explained Miss Thornish. "And *he* taught me. Though he admitted that there was much to be said in favour of the French school with its greater scope for finger play. And particularly for a woman. However he judged it better for me to learn one method thoroughly. Time enough then, he said, to experiment."

"I wish I had been more intimately acquainted with my uncle," said Mr. Develyn thoughtfully. "Do you realise, ma'am, that I do not know him as well as you do? Have not seen him these twenty years past?"

"He was very wise. And upright and generous," said Miss Thornish simply. "But we are putting off time—and I am becoming more and more nervous for I am sadly out of practice. Will the Italian mounting be a serious handicap for you? We could defer the contest until we can procure foils of the French pattern."

"That would be to handicap *you*," returned Mr. Develyn. "And I already have the advantage in height and reach. No, I thank you, I *have* occasionally used the Italian grip and shall, moreover, be thankful to have a perfectly respectable excuse for a poor showing. Do you imagine that you are the only one to feel nervous? Your brother's warning still rings in my ears!"

She laughed. "Oh! That was just his fraternal loyalty. I believe he did not do himself justice. His notions of chivalry would not permit him to exert his full force against a female. Engaging with you is a very different proposition."

Mr. Develyn laughed so much that he gasped for breath while Miss Thornish regarded him with puzzled surprise. Recovering at last, he mopped his eyes and said, "I can only hope that your fencing is less disconcerting than your tongue. You do not, I gather, credit me with a chivalry to match your brother's. But it is less than kind in you to tell me so. Next, I suppose, you will explain that Uncle Miles taught you never to dissemble nor palter with the truth."

That made her blush and stammer out some kind of apology. "You know I did not mean it so! It is just that Geoffrey is only a boy, while you——" She broke off, aware that she was getting more and more entangled in personalities. The amusement still gleamed in his eyes. Impulsively she picked up the foils, resting both hilts on her forearm, and offered him his choice with a quaint little bow. "Let us continue the conversation with these," she suggested, recovering her poise.

The opening phrases of the encounter were naturally cautious, each protagonist more concerned to assess the strength and skill of the other than to score hits. Mr. Develyn, using an unfamiliar weapon, was content to maintain a close guard and allow Miss Thornish to take the lead if she so wished. He had entered upon the bout with some half formed notion of allowing her to score a hit or two out of pure kindness. He soon abandoned it. She was too good a fencer to be deceived by such a childish stratagem and would be very properly furious.

She was, in fact, very good indeed, light and quick on her feet yet so smooth and relaxed that parry, riposte and counter-attack seemed to flow from the flickering blade as though of natural impulse rather than design. But Mr. Develyn was under no misapprehension. The mind that directed the apparently careless invitations, the innocent-seeming parries and swift disengagements was cool and keen as the blade itself. Miss Thornish had learned to make intelligent strategy and, perhaps, a certain degree of acting ability, make up for what she lacked in reach and physical force.

So he was not sorry when, at the end of a brisk engagement lasting some five or six minutes, she sprang back out of distance and lowered her point. She was flushed and breathless, he composed and cool as ever.

"You see?" she queried. "I said I was out of practice!"

"And heaven be duly thanked for it," retorted Mr. Develyn, "else I should be lying a pallid corpse at your feet."

"Slain by a buttoned foil?" she laughed, still rather breathless but plainly gratified.

"And can you imagine the peal that my uncle would have rung over me if I had arrived unshriven in Paradise as a result of his pupil's prowess?"

She smiled, but shook her head. "You know very well that I had no hope of penetrating your guard, even if I had been in good condition. I imagine that with your own chosen weapon you would have been less—defensive?"

He grinned. She was so honest, so eager. To speak less than the truth would be patronising. "I found the grip rather restrictive," he admitted. "It gives strength and control but there is less scope for subtlety. So I deemed it wiser to protect my reputation as best I might rather than embark upon rash attacks that might have given you just the opening you sought."

She nodded. "As I thought. Now where can we procure foils of the French pattern, so that you may teach me the difference in technique?"

"Why, as to that, I daresay my brother Edward still has the pair that he and I used as boys. They would serve very well, being light enough for you to handle easily. I think you would enjoy the added finesse and dexterity that they give, once you had mastered the basic principle. Shall I bring them back with me next week when I take Robin to visit my father?"

"If your brother will be so kind as to lend them. And if *you* do not object to spending your time and energies on my instruction," she added more diffidently.

"I shall look forward to it," he told her. "It is far too long since I indulged in foil play. I had forgotten what an exhilarating exercise it is, and must thank you for a pleasure regained. But upon one condition only. You must wear a mask."

She looked a little dubious. "I have never done so," she said slowly. "Milord did not deem it necessary."

"No doubt he had sufficient confidence in his skill and control," said Mr. Develyn diplomatically. "I have not. Moreover, in *his* hey-day, masks were unheard of. Or perhaps I should rather say they had been forgotten until La Boëssière re-invented them, though in fact the Egyptians used them in their fencing matches many hundreds of years ago. And although I can show you the technique of the fingers, I will not again engage with you unless we are both protected against accident."

She was much inclined to resent this masterful attitude, but she was also very eager to learn the new technique. And what was the good of learning it if one had no opportunity to try it out? A few idle remarks about the dangers of a slip of the foot or a snapping blade, a laughing reference to the old saying that no good fencing master ended his life with two good eyes, and she allowed herself to be persuaded.

Mr. Develyn put up the Italian foils in their case and enquired where his daughter might be. Since her arrival at Saxondene her life had not followed quite the pattern that he had pictured. She did, indeed, spend a good deal of her time riding and walking with him, vividly interested in his plans for improvements and shyly accepting the kindly welcome of tenants and estate workers. But naturally there were many occasions when she could not be with him and on these occasions he discovered an increasing tendency on Robin's part to gravitate towards South Gates.

It had begun naturally enough when her first night

had been passed under its hospitable roof. Mr. Develyn, arriving betimes next day to collect his daughter, had found her curled up in one of Miss Thornish's comfortable chairs, the jade horse in her lap, listening with a rapt expression to some history concerning the beast which had broken off abruptly at his entry. He had begged the narrator to continue but she had said quietly that the tale would keep for another day and that Robin was longing to see the real horse—the sturdy black pony that Mr. Develyn had finally settled upon as a reliable first 'friend'—which was waiting for her in the stables.

Lady Anley and Miss Terbert might have their faults, but between them they had taught Robin good manners. She made no demur at having her story interrupted, only asking shyly if she might *really* come to hear the end of it another day. Upon receiving an assurance to this effect, she thanked Miss Thornish for her kindness without prompting, slipped a hand into her father's and went off very happily to make her pony's acquaintance.

She was hugely tickled to hear that he was called Blackbird and that Papa had thought that a Robin and a Blackbird should be good friends. She laughed aloud, a clear little ripple of joy. Mr. Develyn was guiltily aware that he had never heard it before. Oh! He was right, he *must* be right, that the child's happiness lay here, in the country, with him.

But though Robin and Blackbird were friends from the start there was still many hours that the child must spend alone or with the servants. When her father was engaged on business that would be tedious for a child, what was she to do with herself? Mrs. Johnson assured him that she would come to no harm in Becky's company. Becky was a very good sort of girl, strictly brought up and a cut above the usual type of village girl who went into service. The daughter of a tenant farmer, she would normally have been kept at home to help her mother save that she had two elder sisters. Two, said Mrs. Marlow briskly, was enough. They were forever getting under her feet as it was. She sometimes thought it would be easier to do the tasks herself than to stand over Phoebe and Judith and see that they scrubbed and polished and brewed and baked as it *should* be done. Becky should go into service— so it be *good* service, mind you—and someone else could have the training of her. Her wages would be useful, too, concluded the thrifty lady. Not, with a toss of the head, that the Marlows *needed* to send their daughters out to earn, but with farm prices so bad ever since the wars had ended it was only prudent to add a few guineas to the hoard in the stocking when opportunity offered.

So Becky escaped to a far easier servitude at Saxondene and soon earned Mrs. Johnson's approval by her willingness to turn a hand to whatever was asked of her. With no schoolroom to be waited on she had time and to spare to go with Miss Robin on her rambles abroad and, being country bred, enough good sense to see that she came to no harm, explained the housekeeper.

Which was doubtless perfectly true. But with the onset of winter the weather was scarcely propitious for prolonged rambles. And although Mr. Develyn was anxious for his daughter to have young society, he did not feel that the stolid Becky, however good-humoured and reliable, would be a very stimulating companion. Reluctantly he came to the conclusion that he must set about engaging another governess sooner than he had planned, and decided to consult the Rector as to whether there were other children in the neighbourhood with whom it might be possible to share lessons.

But before he had made any move in this direction, Robin had settled things for herself. In her wanderings with Becky she had several times accompanied the girl to South Gates and had been an interested spectator of the lessons that Miss Thornish gave to two or three of the village girls. No one paid any heed to her, so quiet and still in her corner. Francesca, absorbed in coaxing plodding minds and awkward fingers along the paths of learning, simply took her presence for granted until one day she asked the girls, as was her custom, what they would like to do for the last quarter of an hour. They were always diffident over this. There was much nudging and giggling before one or another would ask if they might play spillikins or have out the musical box. They never wearied of this charming toy which not only tinkled out a gay little tune but also set in motion two tiny figures dressed in Dutch costume who performed a solemn mechanical dance.

On this particular evening, before anyone else had a chance to speak a breathless little voice said suddenly, "Oh! Please, ma'am, won't you play for us?"

Wholly engrossed in the evening's activities, Robin had forgotten her shyness. For a moment Francesca could not think who had spoken. From recent association with Becky there was even a hint of rusticity in the timid little voice. Everyone turned with one accord to stare at Robin who, startled into self-consciousness, blushed furiously, one hand flying to her lips as though to press back the rash words that had been drawn from her almost unawares.

"Do you like music so much, Robin?" asked Francesca gently. And as the child nodded dumbly, too overcome by the sudden centring of attention upon her to find her voice, she turned to the watching girls. "Would you like that?" she asked them.

They looked at one another. It would never have occurred to them to ask such a thing, but the very novelty of the suggestion had its attraction. There were one or two vigorous nods and wide grins. Becky, more confident than the others, said, "Yes please, ma'am. Could you play a jig? Or maybe a waltz?"

Miss Thornish modestly acknowledged that this task should not be beyond her powers and opened the piano. For ten minutes or so she kept her little audience enthralled, playing such popular country airs as she could recall. She played them Corn Rigs, an Irish jig and Hunt the Squirrel, and soon had them nodding and tapping and humming. Rarely had she seen the rosy faces so animated and inwardly applauded Robin's unexpected request. It was plain that music would henceforth become a favorite part of the evening's programme. Finally she played them Come o'er the stream, Charlie, marking the waltz rhythm so strongly that Marian said impulsively, "Oh, ma'am! I wish you could show us how to dance it!"

But this Miss Thornish did not feel herself able to do. "Your parents would not like it," she told them frankly. "They would say it was a waste of time." Also that it was putting foolish notions into heads that were all too easily turned any way, she added mentally, remembering the difficulties she had overcome in winning parental consent for the simple accomplishments that she tried to impart.

The girls went off to the kitchen with Marian for the supper which was a very popular part of the evening's proceedings. It was Robin's usual practice, during this interlude, to bury herself in a book, only raising her head if her hostess addressed her directly, until such time as Becky came back to take her home to bed. Tonight, since Francesca was still seated at the piano, she waited hopefully. Francesca had smiled at the unconscious mimicry in the child's voice as she made her request but she had not missed the urgency that had prompted it. The love of music must be very strong to have broken through Robin's reserve. She began to play again, softly, idly, as though she was only amusing herself. But now her choice was different. She played delicate fragments of Scarlatti, of Couperin and Mozart, slipping easily from one to another as the mood took her, and presently was aware that the shy, silent child had left the refuge of book and easy chair and come softly to stand beside her, watching her hands as she played.

When at last she came to an end, Robin did not thank her, save by a slow contented sigh. It was as though they had been talking together and now the conversation was done. Francesca dared not even risk a direct glance as she said courteously, as to an equal, "You play yourself, perhaps?"

Robin shook her head. "I have had lessons. Miss Terbert was teaching me. It was not playing. Not like *that*." And she nodded worshipfully at Francesca's magnificent Broadwood as though the instrument had of itself produced the sounds which had so entranced her. She drew a deep shuddering breath. "Oh! If only *you* would teach me!"

Francesca was completely taken aback. She had no least intention of becoming closely involved with the Develyns. To be good neighbours was enough. Any woman would have offered the hospitality that she had shown this poor little brat on her first arrival. Then it had been easy enough to tolerate her presence at the girls' classes. No doubt about it she was lonely and half the time one forgot she was there. But this was a very different matter. Her prickly pride was already astir at the very notion of giving music lessons to Mr. Develyn's daughter. Yet the child's appeal was natural enough. She had heard Becky and Marian and their friends ask to be taught a variety of arts, from the proper laundering of lace to the making of pork puddings. What more reasonable than that she, in her turn, should ask to be taught what she so dearly longed to learn? And was not her need, in a different way, as great as theirs?

Francesca did not think it would be easy to explain to Robin that she was not quite in the same class as the other girls. She hedged.

"Won't you play for me?" she suggested, expecting diffidence—mock-modesty—probably a refusal.

Robin's eyes widened. They were grey eyes, very like her father's. In their present intensity of excitement they looked almost black. "Me? On *that* piano?" she breathed.

Francesca smiled and got up to put a cushion on the stool she had been using, leaving the little girl to settle herself comfortably, and sat down to listen.

The apologetic flutterings that she had anticipated were totally absent. Robin tried one or two notes, a few chords, a scale, tentatively at first but with growing confidence and the air of one listening for the voice of a beloved friend. Then without further experiment she launched into the opening movement of that Beethoven sonata which was to be known to later generations as the 'Moonlight'.

As a musical performance it was lamentable. Playing from memory a composition that she did not even know very well, there were constant mistakes and hesitations. But the rapt absorption on the solemn young face, the fierce little frown when she played wrong notes or could not recapture some particular phrase, might have won favour even in the composer's eyes. If Francesca had been a little disappointed by the ambitious nature of the child's choice, she soon realised her error. Robin had forgotten she was there. It was not with an audience, with possible praise or compliment, that *this* performer was concerned.

Slow amusement gleamed in Francesca's eyes to be followed by a glimmer of understanding. Had not she herself found comfort in music making after the scandal that had shattered the ordered pattern of her girlhood? It seemed that for Robin music had offered a world of her own, an escape from the loneliness and the dullness of her restricted days.

The movement stumbled to its close. The pianist heaved a despairing sigh and said sadly, "I know just how it *should* sound, only my fingers won't go right. It's beautiful, isn't it? But sort of sorrowful, too."

For once Francesca found herself at a loss. The brisk, good-humored criticism that she was accustomed to bestow upon Marian or Becky was obviously out of place in this situation. Yet she was herself a musician and her artistic integrity forbade her to praise what had been so badly performed. While she yet sought for words that might be truthful without being too lowering, Robin said simply, "*You* could help me to get it right."

There was neither cajolery nor pleading in the young voice. It was a quiet statement of truth, asking nothing, expecting nothing. Yet it was also the appeal of one musician to another. And before Francesca could answer, the child suddenly betrayed her youthful vulnerability, saying sorrowfully, "We haven't even *got* a piano at home."

That, at least, Francesca could answer. "I am sure your Papa will buy you one when he understands how badly you want it," she consoled. "Meanwhile you may come and play mine, if Papa will agree to it. And I will help you as best I can, though I cannot of course undertake to give you regular lessons."

She dared not promise too much. Though her dealings with Mr. Develyn had been perfectly friendly since Robin's arrival, they were in no sense intimate. No doubt he was much occupied with estate business and now that hunting had begun his time was further taken up, both with the sport itself and with the easy going hospitality associated with it. Perhaps it was not surprising that he had never fulfilled his half-promise to engage in fencing practice with her. But Francesca, unduly sensitive on this head, thought it equally possible that he had decided against closer acquaintance. There had been time by now for him to hear such versions of her past history as were current in the

neighbourhood. If he accepted them at face value—
if he had learned that she still was not received by
the really high sticklers—he would scarcely wish his
innocent young daughter to be thrust into constant
association with her.

She wished that Becky would make haste over her
supper and come to collect her charge. Robin, already
aglow with an eagerness that had transformed her
whole personality, was obviously not going to be
fobbed off with vague talk of 'one day soon'.

It was at this point that Brandon Hornby tapped on
the door to tell her that Mr. Develyn would like to
speak with her. Well thank goodness for that, thought
Francesca, concealing her amusement at her old friend's
air of deep disapprobation.

Since his active employment as courier and escort
had virtually come to an end with the building of
South Gates, Brandon had found a niche for himself
in the world of letters. The facility with languages which
had proved so useful on their travels was now chan-
nelled into quieter ways. He had as much work as he
could handle in supplying accurate and scholarly trans-
lations to a publishing house of some repute. It had
sometimes occurred to Francesca that it was a strange
occupation for one who, in the early years of their
acquaintance, had seemed so much a man of action.
In addition to being a first rate horseman and pretty
useful with his fists, Brandon was the very finest shot
she had ever seen. Even Lord Finmore acknowledged
his superiority in this field. And while, in view of their
extensive travels, his fluency in modern languages might
seem natural enough, she did wonder where he had
acquired his knowledge of classical Greek and Latin.

Though his modest earnings made him independent he was quite willing to live at South Gates as long as Francesca had need of his wife's services as chaperone, and she knew that he still held himself responsible for her welfare. That responsibility had even brought him some measure of comfort during that grim period following his lordship's death.

Francesca had never known what persuasions the Earl had used to beguile the Hornbys into her service, save that they so plainly regarded him as second only to their God. When he had died, at Finmore, Brandon had mourned in some bitter private hell of his own because he had not been there to serve and tend his idol to the last. He had lost weight, grown terse and tetchy. The jealous supervision that he had exercised over her comings and goings had been almost more than she could endure, had it not been for the sympathy she felt for him in his desolation. Intuitively she had understood. Her safe keeping was the sole task that he could still perform for his dead master.

Things had been a little better of late. A particularly exacting piece of work had successfully distracted his mind and the need to keep a watchful eye on the new master of Saxondene had diverted some of his attention from Francesca, though if Mr. Develyn strayed by so much as a hair's breadth from customary usage she was inevitably the first to hear of it. So far the kindest thing he had found to say of the newcomer was that at least he wasn't above listening to advice from those who knew better than he did. But certain reminiscences had shown that Brandon was well aware of his old master's fondness for Mr. Develyn.

Perhaps this knowledge served the gentleman in good

stead upon this occasion, since Brandon was perfectly capable of informing unseasonably late callers that Miss Thornish had retired for the night. Evidently Mr. Develyn stood sufficiently high in his good graces to be admitted at nine o'clock.

"Why, of course, Brand. Pray invite him to step up here if he will be so kind. He is just the person we wanted, isn't he?" she added to Robin. But she glanced guiltily up at the clock. It was certainly rather late for that young lady to be out of her bed.

But Mr. Develyn had not come in search of his errant daughter. In fact he seemed mildly surprised at finding her in Miss Thornish's drawing room. He had come to suggest that as severe frost had caused the cancellation of next day's meet perhaps Miss Thornish would be so kind as to indulge him with a little foil play.

Miss Thornish would be delighted to do so. In fact Francesca was surprised at the sudden lightening of her spirits. It seemed quite simple after all to put Robin's request before him, quite natural to hear him endorse her own suggestions, to advise over the choice of a piano. When he further suggested that, provided she was not allowed to become a nuisance, Robin could perfectly well dispense with Becky's escort to South Gates and could run in and out as her hostess permitted, she finally dismissed the last suspicion that Mr. Develyn thought badly of her and it was in a mood of happy anticipation that she appointed eleven o'clock next morning as a convenient time for their engagement.

Since riding was out of the question while the frost held she was not really surprised when Robin arrived alone considerably before that hour. She reminded the rapt musician that she would be turned out when Papa came and left her to improve her acquaintance with the Broadwood while she herself attended to her domestic responsibilities, occasionally strolling into the drawing room to offer a word of advice or to draw the pianist's attention to one or two works that she thought might appeal to her before going up to her room to change her charming morning gown for the masculine attire more suited to fencing.

Now, watching Mr. Develyn replace the foils on their shelf she was aware of a pleasant contentment. Not in an age had she passed so entertaining a forenoon. What a pity that there would be no possibility of a repetition for some time. She found herself hoping that Mr. Develyn's visit to his paternal home would not be unduly prolonged. Robin, she told him, had gone off to the stables to have a talk with Blackbird and to watch the young vixen, Reyna, being fed. They speculated for a while on the difficulties that Reyna would encounter in returning to the wild. Mr. Develyn, with a distinctive twinkle, strongly advocated the locking up of the chicken coops when this event occurred. "For she will surely make for familiar ground and the places that she associates with food as soon as she feels the pinch of hunger," he pointed out.

Francesca confessed to having contemplated putting some food out for the creature. "For the first few nights, just till she becomes accustomed."

Mr. Develyn shook his head. "Unwise," he insisted. "It would probably be taken by some other night prowler. And hunger will supply the strongest spur to the beast's natural instincts which must be brought into play if she is to have a chance of survival."

Francesca sighed but admitted that he was probably in the right of it.

"And if she is full-fed when you release her, short commons won't harm her for a day or two," he comforted, as he shrugged himself into his jacket and went off to find Robin.

Seven

Christmas came and went, to be followed by a long spell of exceptionally mild dry weather. Ploughing and sowing went on apace and the hunting people gloomily predicted an early end to the season. Mr. Develyn and his daughter spent Christmas in Town with Lady Anley where Robin was petted and praised and showered with costly and elegant gifts until she was in a fair way to being spoiled to death—if only she had cared for such things. She behaved very well, showing sincere affection for Grandmama and displaying proper gratitude for all the treasures bestowed upon her. Only Papa knew that for Robin the highlight of the London week was the visit that the pair of them paid to the famous pianoforte showrooms in Great Pulteney Street, where she was allowed to choose the instrument that was to be Papa's Christmas gift to her.

For one thing Mr. Develyn was rather ashamedly grateful. Under Grandmama's roof once more, Robin reverted to her London manners, speaking only when directly addressed. So it chanced that no mention was made of the increasing part that Miss Thornish had come to play in her life. Lady Anley was distressed that no governess had as yet been engaged to replace Miss Terbert, but Mr. Develyn was able to reassure her on this head. Mr. Whittingham's orphaned niece had just come to make her home with him at the Rectory and it had been arranged that, for a trial period, she should come daily to teach Robin her lessons. She was a little young for the position—barely eighteen—but she had been carefully educated and was thankful to find genteel employment so close to her new home. Lady Anley was dubious, pointing out the advantages of a resident governess, preferably an older woman, but her son-in-law said that he and Robin did very well on their own and added bluntly that he thought a resident governess would be an embarrassment in a masculine household.

"She wouldn't always be teaching young Robin," he pointed out, "or taking her for walks and supervising her practice and such. And what the deuce should I do with her in between whiles?"

Lady Anley was much struck by the good sense of this argument. Especially if the governess chanced to be a designing sort of female. Robert wouldn't be the first lonely male to be taken in *that* kind of trap; the womanly sympathy—the subtle flattery—the deference to masculine superiority. On the other hand, was there not equal danger in the alternative arrangement? Robert was not yet forty. So far as she knew he had had no dealings with women since the loss of his wife, but he might well be susceptible to the innocent charms of an eighteen-year-old.

"What is Miss Marsden like?" she enquired.

Mr. Develyn looked blank. "Like? Why, just like any other girl of good family at that age. Mild and milky. But pleasantly spoken and fond of music—which, of course, recommends her to Robin. I doubt, however, if we shall keep her very long. From what her uncle hinted I believe she has an understanding with a young gentleman in holy orders, though their betrothal and marriage must wait upon his preferment. But if Robin likes her and she stays until the child is of an age to go to school, the arrangement would seem to suit both parties."

Lady Anley could not see that Robin's liking had any bearing on the case, but her mind was relieved of its immediate anxiety. She ventured one more question.

"Have you ever thought of marrying again, Robert?"

How did one tell one's mama-in-law that one adventure into matrimony had been more than sufficient? Shocked and shamed by her daughter's elopement, she had been strongly inclined to take his part and had blamed his wife more, perhaps, than was strictly just. But since Helena's death her mother had not so much forgiven her sins and follies as glossed them over beneath a veil of easy oblivion. Death was, at least, respectable. For Robert, whose whole life had been twisted out of true by his wife's betrayal, it was not quite so easy. And more than ever, of late, since he had savoured the satisfaction of an ordered and useful existence, had he come to regret the wasted years. Marry again? He rather thought not! But he could scarcely expect Lady Anley to enter into his sentiments. He smiled at her gravely. With her head tilted a little to one side beneath that ornate creation of lace and velvet blossoms that she called a cap, she reminded him irresistibly of the vividly coloured humming birds that he had so much admired during his South American expedition. The resemblance extended even to temperament he thought amusedly, remembering the way in which the gay little creatures had flitted from flower to flower.

"Let us say that I have scarcely been much in the way of meeting marriageable females," he evaded gently. "And at the moment my daughter satisfies my need for feminine society."

She was not entirely reassured, but he had gone on to speak of other matters and it did not seem possible to press her enquiries further.

Both father and daughter were well content to return to Saxondene. For Robin it meant the end of holiday and the beginning of regular lessons, but it also meant free access to the South Gates Broadwood—far superior to Grandmama's piano which, in any case, she was only permitted to use during the mornings. Soon, very soon now, she would have her own, which she could play whenever she wished, provided—for Papa, beginning to know his daughter, was no longer so rash or so wholesale in his promises as in earlier days—that Miss Marsden reported satisfactory effort in her general studies and that Blackbird was not neglected.

Mr. Develyn had found Town life surprisingly tedious. It seemed strange, with so much to see and to do, so many invitations to renew acquaintance with former friends, but there could be no denying that time passed much more quickly in the country. At Saxondene the days never seemed long enough for all the things he wished to do. Ruefully he recalled that he would have to spend another week in Town at the beginning of March when he was engaged to address the Society of Antiquaries. It was a great honour and he had been duly appreciative when he received the invitation, but it was a pity that it meant tearing himself away from Saxondene yet again.

Between the long, slow-paced farming considerations, the occasional day's hunting, riding with Robin, fencing with Francesca and evenings divided between estate work and the preparation of his talk to the Antiquaries, the days passed both pleasantly and swiftly. Only one embarrassing incident threatened to mar the harmony that prevailed between South Gates and the big house, and that was, in truth, so absurd that even Robert simply had to laugh.

It would be the last meet of the season but it had been a splendid day—the kind of day when everything he did went right. Rustic was fit as a flea and jumping like one, proportionate to his size, and at the end of a famous three mile point he found himself very well placed with the leaders. Then their fox swerved sharply, hounds over-ran, and checked, just short of his own south lodge.

Scent was poor in the dry, sunny much-used lane. Sir Lucas was a Master who never fussed his hounds. He let them alone, and they cast themselves. Two minutes later Mr. Develyn would thankfully have surrendered his favourable position to anyone who desired it, as a triumphant wave of black and tan and white poured up his south drive and put to ground at the door-sill of the shed that sheltered the captive vixen, Reyna.

Most people knew of the creature's existence but naturally no fox-hunting man had so much as dreamed of Miss Thornish exercising it, dog fashion, on a lead. Hounds could scarcely be blamed for their natural error. Fortunately it was already late. Horses were jaded—one or two stragglers had already slipped away home—and after the excellent sport they had enjoyed, especially that last magnificent burst, no one really minded that the day should end with the best joke of the season. Mr. Develyn's face might be red, but his fellows exploded into gales of laughter and though he was too new to country ways to realise it the legend created that day would be remembered by generations yet unborn.

Sir Lucas, his face wooden with the effort to stifle his own amusement, drew off his reluctant pack. Mr. Develyn, putting a good face on the thing, offered hospitality. Grooms came up to take the steaming horses and Mr. Develyn, with a darkling look at the shed that concealed the cause of his confusion, led the way indoors.

His comments to Francesca next day were pithy in the extreme and the frank amusement in the hazel eyes was scarcely calculated to mollify. A certain degree of intimacy had grown up between them during the fencing lessons. When one was pupil and the other instructor there was no room for polite evasions and discreet dissemblings, and the habit of frank comment, once established, had tended to colour the whole of their dealings together. Mr. Develyn had come to rely on Francesca's local knowledge and also consulted her

freely about Robin's welfare. It was at her suggestion
that Robin now attended a weekly dancing class and
was beginning to make a few acquaintances of her own
age. While frankly admitting to ignorance about bringing up children, Francesca claimed that she knew a
good deal from personal experience about how *not* to
do it, and urged that learning to mix easily with one's
contemporaries was of first importance. There was
nothing more miserable for a child than being 'different'. Mr. Develyn, expounding *his* ideas on his
daughter's upbringing, listing the advantages and disadvantages of school as against education at home,
found in her an attentive listener, perhaps all the more
acceptable in that she offered no advice at all but simply
allowed him to talk himself out.

She listened to him now as he described yesterday's
fiasco. His own appreciation of the ridiculous helped
him to tell the story well despite his indignation at
being made to look like a fool by what he described
as her "misplaced charity."

"I shall be thankful to see the last of that evil-
smelling brute," he finished forthrightly. "When do you
propose to set her at large?"

Francesca was not in the least crushed by these
strictures. "If we are to talk of smells," she said
sweetly, "I doubt if your library smelt particularly
sweet yesterday with a dozen or so extremely horsey
gentlemen congregated about the fires; while a discerning dog fox would probably find Reyna's scent positively alluring. But as for setting her free—if yesterday
really was the last hunt of the season, then I shall
loose her tonight."

He looked at her curiously, a little surprised that she

should yield so readily to his demand, a little perturbed lest he might have expressed himself more forcibly than was courteous. "You will not be sorry to see her go?" he suggested tentatively.

She shrugged. "Perhaps not. I suppose it was foolish in me to foster her as I did. Geoffrey certainly thought so. But as you know, there is that in my past history that begets in me sharp sympathy with any young creature cast unprotected upon a hostile world. I yielded to a sentimental impulse where Reyna was concerned and can only trust that my interference has done no irreparable harm."

"Since without your interference the cub must have died, you may surely acquit yourself on that count," said Mr. Develyn drily. "Thanks to you she has survived to maturity and now you propose to set her free. So why this heart searching? You are refining too much on a very trivial matter."

"I know," she admitted. "But I also know how it feels to be utterly bereft and desperate. In my case your uncle extended a strong protective hand to raise and shelter me. And not even he could fully restore——" She broke off. "I am becoming maudlin," she said crisply. "Set it down to spring sickness. You have my promise that you shall be relieved of Reyna's obnoxious presence very shortly."

He could not leave it at that. Save for the information in his uncle's letter he knew nothing of her past though she seemed to take it for granted that he did. And he was conscious of a deep interest that was not just idle curiosity. What circumstances had moulded her into the unusual creature that she was? He thought of the comradeship that had grown up between them during the past months. Honest to a fault, wise, understanding, astringent by turns, yet using a tolerant humour in all her judgements, he had come to value her opinion sincerely. Now he said slowly, "Of your dealings with my uncle I know nothing—save that he valued you above all other women. In his farewell letter he told me that he had offered you his hand in marriage. If *you* choose to tell me more I would esteem myself honoured by your confidence but naturally the decision must rest with you."

She had swung round sharply at his opening remarks, plainly startled that he should be privy to a secret that she had thought locked in her own bosom. Despite the fortitude that she had learned Francesca was but human. There had been moments when, stung by cruel snubs and social ostracism, she had found consolation in the thought of how she *could* have triumphed over her enemies. Countess of Finmore! Aunt Maud and all those other haughty dames who, in their self righteousness, had set themselves up as her judges would have been all obsequious civility. But not even to her own brother had she betrayed the truth and it had never occurred to her that the Earl himself might have done so.

She turned back to the window and stood gazing out into the sunny garden. "Since you know so much, you had best know it all," she said quietly, "for his lordship's offer was but the generous impulse of a great heart. The affection between us was warm and sincere but it was not of the kind that makes for a successful marriage. Though he would never admit it, I believe he was very grateful for my refusal."

For the second time within six months she rehearsed

the story of her meeting with the Earl of Finmore. She told it briefly, unemotionally, almost as though speaking of strangers, and Mr. Develyn listened in silence. She had reached the point in her story where his lordship had taken her to Rome so that she might have the benefit of the best possible musical tuition.

"I do not want you to think that I was unhappy," she said, very positively. "I was surrounded by every possible comfort. My days were full of interest, my singing lessons exacting and absorbing. His lordship was a delightful companion. But naturally he had a number of friends of his own generation and a great many interests into which a raw child of seventeen could not be expected to enter. Since, moreover, he was extremely particular that I should observe the rules of conventional behaviour, the hours that he could spend with me were strictly limited. At that time I could not speak fluent Italian so I was often very lonely. Mrs. Hornby is the kindest creature but there were times when I yearned for younger, gayer society. There was one particular occasion when I had been sitting at the window in my apartment watching the people in the street. It was a very beautiful evening in early summer and some distinguished personage was giving a grand party. Carriage after carriage went by, moving very slowly, so great was the press of traffic, with everyone staring and exclaiming at the dresses and the jewels and I staring with the rest and wishing that I, too, was going to the party. Only that morning, when I had been buying some muslins more suited to the Italian climate, I had seen just such a gown as I would have chosen to wear."

She turned to face him and now she was smiling

reminiscently. "I can see it still. The tiny heart-shaped bodice, the skirt a cloud of white tulle embroidered with pink rosebuds; even the lace mittens that went with it, a matching rosebud at each wrist. Goodness! *What* a figure of fun I should have looked—tricked out like a maypole and almost as tall! But I had lost my heart to it and I fear that I was shedding a few ridiculous tears at the thought that I should never wear such a gown, never go to parties like other girls, when his lordship walked in on me. In justice to myself let me say that I was not expecting him. Quite unexpectedly he had been offered the use of a box at the opera and had thought I might enjoy the treat."

Her eyes met Robert's. "You know what your uncle was. It did not take him five minutes to have the whole sorry tale out of me. Unfortunately he had never before seen me in tears. It is not a weakness to which I am much addicted," she put in defensively, "and he was much affected. *That* was when he made me an offer. If I cared to marry him I could go to all the parties I chose—though *not*, he was careful to stipulate, in white tulle and pink rosebuds." Her mouth softened. Her whole expression grew brooding, tender. "He desired marriage no more than he had ever desired it. He offered me his name and his rank as one offers a toy to a child, to dry its tears."

"And you refused him," reminded Robert gently.

For a moment she did not seem to hear him, still dwelling in that long past moment of time. Then she shook off her memories and looked up at him, smiling. "I did. And I vow there was gratitude in his eye, though he always denied it."

"Do you still yearn for dress parties?"

"White tulle and pink rosebuds? No, indeed! Though I *do* regret that I have had so little opportunity of dancing, an exercise that I much enjoy. For the rest— I have seen and done so much, thanks to your uncle, that other girls have missed, that I count myself very fortunate. It is only very rarely, I promise you, that I am overcome by such nostalgia as I have permitted you to glimpse today. As I said, you must set it down to the restlessness perfectly natural in the spring of the year. I think, perhaps, I have lingered too long at South Gates. It is time to be done with mourning my dear lord. Time to be off on my travels again."

Eight

"In any event I shall have to be in Town for a full sennight—perhaps longer. So if you should consent to my suggestion I could drive you up in my chaise, escort you to the Opera—a theatre or two—whatever you choose. I make no doubt you will have shopping and visiting enough to beguile the hours when I must desert you for my own affairs. I mean to put up at Fenton's for convenience sake. It is close at hand for the arrangement of my exhibits and I have always found it perfectly comfortable. There is no reason why you should not engage rooms there yourself, since you will have Mrs. Hornby to play propriety, unless, of course, you prefer something a little more dashing. Do you not agree that my prescription might serve to allay the restlessness of which you were complaining the other day?"

Francesca's eyes were lowered to the foil that she was absently flexing between her hands. The invitation was more tempting than he guessed. Capable and self-reliant as she had learned to be, she knew very well that a presentable male escort made all the difference to one's comfort on such a visit as he proposed, and she was inclined to believe that Mr. Develyn would be just such an escort—unobtrusive but firm in ensuring her enjoyment. Only the uncomfortable thought that the invitation had been prompted by pity prevented her from accepting with an unbecoming eagerness.

"Surely you did not take my idle plaint so much to heart?" she said lightly. "You must know that all females are prone to sentimental recollections when the long spring evenings remind us of the speed at which the years are passing. You must not dream of putting yourself out on my account."

"I don't," he retorted coolly. "On my last two visits to London I have been quite shockingly bored. Since this is a business visit, courtesy does not insist that I stay at Anley House—and I am taking appropriate measures to counter the possibility of boredom in my leisure hours."

She glanced up, and laughed. "You are very like your uncle when you speak *so*," she told him. "He too, kept a rough tongue for those whom he counted his friends. For toad-eaters and time-servers he used a purring suavity that was venomous. I am gratified that you count me sufficiently a friend to be a possible antidote to boredom. Let us hope," with a gleam of wicked mirth, "that I do not become too flown with conceit at such flattery. It would be a sad come-down if, in my efforts to prove entertaining, I were to set Society by the ears—as you must be aware I am accustomed to doing."

There was a hint of challenge in the last remark, despite the airy nonsense. He met it equably. "Let us agree that you are an abandoned hussy and quite past praying for, shall we? If you choose to create riot and rumpus it is very much your own affair, though I do *trust* I shall not be obliged to come and bail you out. However you may perfectly rely upon me to do so, should it become necessary, though if you are taken up in *that* rig I shall certainly refer to you as Mr. Francis Thornish, if only to spare the blushes of the Watch."

She grinned. "Unlikely. It is sad to reflect that I have outgrown the youthful high spirits that might once have prompted me to perpetrate just such a hoax. If you are really serious in your invitation I shall be very happy to accept of it. Only, no Mrs. Hornby. I'll bring my maid, but I am past the age of needing a chaperone, and Catherine is past the age of dancing attendance on what she patiently calls my 'whimsical energies'."

Mr. Develyn frowned. An abigail was all very well, but for a single lady to stay unchaperoned in the same hotel as her attentive escort was beyond the line of being pleasing. He said so—quite uncompromisingly.

"Oh! Nonsense! I'll wear sober gowns and even a cap if you like. I haven't yet taken to wearing one but perhaps it's time that I did. Everyone will think I'm your maiden aunt and we'll brush through with never a hint of scandal."

"You'll do no such thing," he told her roundly. "Do you imagine I want all my friends commiserating with me on the shocking frump that I am taking about? And enquiring if you are some indigent relative or one of the mummies I dug up in Gizeh? No, really, Francesca, that's asking too much of any man. If I know you at all—and I'm beginning to—you would let that madcap sense of humour run away with you and rig yourself out as such a figure of fun that I should be hard put to it not to laugh in your face—or shake you as you deserved."

Francesca bubbled with laughter, a low, delicious chuckling sound. "You are indeed beginning to know me! The thought *had* just flashed across my mind— when I spoke of sober gowns, you know—that I might borrow from Catherine's wardrobe. And since she is three inches shorter than I and a good deal plumper, the result *might* not have been all that a gentleman could desire. Very well then. I will be docile and obedient. Not my poor Catherine—she so dislikes the noise and bustle of Town—but I will put up at Grillon's or Brown's. And no cap, either. I will do my best to measure up to your sartorial standards and not to disgrace you in the eyes of your acquaintance."

"My uncle should have taught you that it is forward and improper to angle for compliments," said Mr. Develyn severely. "You will have none from me by such methods. Can you be ready by Thursday?"

She agreed to this and they discussed the theatrical attractions currently available in the metropolis. These were likely to be limited as the season was not yet begun. Mr. Develyn regretted that he would not have time for another fencing lesson before Thursday. In view of his impending absence there was a good deal to be done so that all should be left in good order. "Not that Shires is not perfectly capable," he admitted, a trifle shamefaced, "but I like to see into things for myself."

She nodded, and made no comment. But she thought that the Earl had chosen wisely in his disposition of Saxondene. He had known his man. Kentish folk were slow to make up their minds and slower still to speak them but already one or two trickles of opinion had reached Francesca. In the main they were favourable. The new master was an ill man to cozen but fair enough if you did right by him. In country parlance, and after only six months' acquaintance, that was high praise.

She murmured her regrets for the interruption in the fencing lessons which had become a regular and enjoyable feature of her day.

"I shall miss them too," agreed Mr. Develyn. "It is a pity, though, that you are so apt a pupil. Soon I shall be forced to defend myself in earnest. Perhaps then you will find me less willing to oblige you with a practice bout."

For once he had the satisfaction of putting her out of countenance. She blushed, stammered and disclaimed at the rare and unexpected praise in a fashion quite unworthy of the cool and poised Miss Thornish, until he took pity on her embarrassment and turned the subject by asking if anything had been seen or heard of the vixen, Reyna, since her liberation.

She shook her head. "At least, Paderson said she had gone with one of his ducks—but *you* know Paderson. He had not even the wit to tell a plausible tale. I expect they ate the duck and hoped to trick me into making good its price."

"Which you did," said Mr. Develyn with calm conviction.

She eyed him with some resentment. It was all very well to say that he was beginning to know her, but this was carrying it *too* far.

"Well—yes," she admitted reluctantly, "but not until I'd told him I knew it was all a hum and that he need not try the same trick again. They are so very poor, you see. I know it is mostly idleness and lack of management, but—what is the price of a duck to me? I expect Mrs. Paderson was glad to be able to give the children a good dinner for once."

"It is to be hoped that she did, since Paderson probably expended your bounty on strong ale at the Three Pigeons. No other news? No sanguinary scenes in the poultry yard?"

She was very pleased to assure him that there was nothing of *that* sort, and he left her in a mood of happy anticipation such as she had not known in months.

Her account of Reyna did not tally with certain scraps of information which had reached him. It seemed that the vixen had been seen on several occasions in the vicinity of her old home. She had not committed any depredations and had appeared healthy and full-fed. But Robert doubted if she would long survive her liberation since all reports were agreed that she seemed to have lost her natural fear of man. She would not allow herself to be approached or touched but neither did she make off at the approach of strangers. He could not help feeling that it would be just as well to have Francesca safely away to London before the inevitable fate overtook her ill-starred fosterling.

The week that she spent in Town was even more

enjoyable than Francesca had anticipated, and this despite the fact that they were offered nothing outstanding in the way of theatrical entertainment. She had hoped to hear Madame Malibran whom she had met and admired in Italy, but the popular singer had returned to Paris and though her successor had a fine voice she was less gifted as an actress. The plays, too, were of indifferent character. Mr. Develyn said ruefully that he now understood why the Society of Antiquaries should be willing to listen to *him*, since every other form of entertainment in Town was certainly at low ebb.

But Francesca had lived secluded so long that the very fact of putting on a pretty gown and going out in the evening with a masculine escort was quite sufficient to elevate her spirits. And however mediocre the play that they had witnessed, the informal supper parties afterwards were wholly delightful. They would discuss the performance and the actors, compare notes on the day's activities and wander into a dozen conversational by-paths so that sometimes it was very late indeed before Mr. Develyn restored his guest to her lodging.

Francesca also enjoyed a positive orgy of shopping, resolutely closing her mind to an inner voice which enquired when next she would have the occasion to wear such festal raiment. The intent look in Mr. Develyn's eye upon beholding her in the green gown which she had worn on the first evening had not escaped her. That look had betrayed some surprise and, she thought, admiration. The gown, of heavy matt silk, had been admirably chosen to set off a lady whose chief assets, if one had grown accustomed to the magnificence of those dark-lashed hazel eyes, were a slender elegant figure and a creamy, magnolia-smooth skin. But though rarely worn, it had been bought almost two years ago. She could do better than *that*! That gleam of surprise had put her on her mettle and she meant to astonish him. No doubt he would think her wildly extravagant, but that, after all, was no bread and butter of his.

Nevertheless she *did* hesitate before she bought the brocaded yellow gauze. Setting aside the fact that it was quite shockingly expensive, it was not at all suitable for a quiet evening at the theatre. It was clearly intended to grace a ballroom—and a pretty grand one at that. But never, since the rosebud-embroidered tulle that had once entranced her girlish heart had she so desired a dress. And it was almost sinfully becoming.

She studied her reflection in the long mirror—and wondered why one always appeared more becoming in a modiste's mirror than in one's own. Something to do with cunningly placed candles perhaps. She turned from side to side, watching with fascinated eyes how the colour changed from palest gold to glowing amber.

"The brocading is done with the new chameleon silk, madam," volunteered the modiste. "Quite the *dernier cri*, I assure you. Though this tulle, worked with lamy à la Taglioni, is extremely fashionable too, and lapis lazuli a very fashionable shade."

But blue was not Francesca's colour, and tulle, remembering his late lordship's remarks about circus dancers on horseback, was perhaps a little too floating, a little too fussy, especially when worked with a pattern of silver thread.

She succumbed to the temptation of the golden gown

and paid Madame Lavinia's extortionate bill without a
blink. By the time that she had found matching slippers
—for it would have been positively sacrilegious to tar-
nish that golden glow with commonplace black satin—
a fan of old, creamy ivory, pierced and painted with
golden irises and a delicate circlet of topaz to set in
her hair, she had spent the price of a new carriage,
she reflected. And all for a whim—since the gown
might never be worn. Opening all the packages and reviewing her purchases in the sober comfort of her
hotel bedchamber, she judged the extravagance well
worth while.

She spent the next day quietly, driving out of Town
to visit her former governess, now retired and living in
Whetstone. It was the day when Mr. Develyn was to
give his lecture to the Antiquaries and she had thankfully accepted his suggestion that she should make the
journey in comfort in his chaise. She had laughed at
his insistence that she leave betimes on her return
journey, vowing that nowadays Finchley Common was
as safe as Bond Street—perhaps safer, having regard
to the press of traffic in the latter thoroughfare. But
she had found his concern for her safety touching, and
though she had only teased him, pretending regret that
she had not thought to bring her pistols to Town and
enquiring if he would advise her to hire outriders to
escort her safely to her destination, she was aware of
a warm feeling of comfort when she recalled his careful
instructions to the postilion who was to have charge
of her journey.

The afternoon with Miss Armes passed pleasantly
enough. There was a placid affection between them
though no great intimacy. Today she had much to tell

of her week's gaiety and the shopping she had done. Mr. Develyn's name occurred frequently, inducing Miss Armes to enquire into his relations with her former pupil. If she did not find the answer wholly to her liking she knew better than to expostulate. Francesca was no longer a schoolgirl on her probation but a grown woman of determined character. Devoutly Miss Armes hoped that the association between the pair had passed unnoticed. To be spending every evening in each other's company must inevitably cause undesirable comment, however open and innocent the meetings. Thankfully she remembered that Town must still be very thin of company, a view that Francesca, when adroitly questioned, readily confirmed, and turned instead to the non-controversial topic of archaeology.

Francesca was surprised to discover how much she was able to impart. She had not realised just how much knowledge she had picked up during those leisurely supper time sessions. Since Mr. Develyn's days had been spent in selecting and arranging the objects which he wished to exhibit and in polishing and rehearsing his address, he had naturally spoken a good deal about his work. She had not always been able to follow the details of his exposition since his enthusiasm was apt to carry him into scientific realms beyond her understanding, but she had found it absorbingly interesting.

Listening to one whom she remembered as being far from studious discoursing at length on the proper methods to be used in the exploration of ancient sites, Miss Armes did not know whether to be amazed or amused. Francesca spoke approvingly of the methods used by Winckelman in his study of Pompeii, adding

that it was a sad pity that the place should have been
so ruthlessly ransacked by earlier treasure seekers.
There was something called a Three Age System de-
vised by a Danish scholar whose name escaped her.
It helped you to classify the objects you found. After
all—men wouldn't have used stone or bone for their
tools, would they, if bronze or iron had been available?
But her greatest enthusiasm was reserved for a Mr.
Thomas Jefferson, the third President of the United
States. It seemed that this gentleman's report on some
Indian burial ground was a model of objective obser-
vation and deduction.

Miss Armes, who had never been able to induce her
pupil to learn so much as the names of the kings of
England—or, indeed, to listen to any kind of history
lesson with more than submissive patience—was filled
with admiration for the persuasive powers of Mr. Robert Develyn. She could not help feeling that it was the
personality rather than the subject matter which had
made such a marked impression, and set herself to
discover the state of Francesca's feelings towards him.
She came up against a blank wall. The girl—for so
Miss Armes still regarded her though she must be close
on twenty nine—was perfectly happy to talk about her
new friend, full of praise for the way in which he had
shouldered his new responsibilities and for the kindness
which he had shown to her, personally, this past
week. But her eyes were clear and candid, her voice
dispassionate, her colour steady. No hint of the tender
passion there, decided Miss Armes, deeply disappointed.

A spinster herself, she would have liked to enlarge
to her guest upon all the disadvantages of that state.
Mr. Develyn must be accounted an excellent match

and Francesca obviously held him in some regard. She longed to advise the girl to make a push to engage his affections. As the onlooker who best sees the game, she knew just how it should be done. But such a hint might be resented and would certainly put an end to further confidences. She said temperately that Mr. Develyn sounded to be quite an asset to the neighbourhood, and hoped that she might have the pleasure of making his acquaintance when she paid her annual visit to South Gates at the end of June. They talked for a little while about their arrangements for this event, planning the excursions that they might make if the weather proved favourable.

No highwayman disturbed the peace of Francesca's return, but her thoughts were not happy ones. The comfort of the chaise, the spring-time charm of the countryside, no longer served to elevate her spirits. Dear Armi! the pet name had evolved from the schoolgirl contraction of the governess's name and that same schoolgirl's lamentable pronunciation of the French 'ami' in years long past. Francesca thought of her now with kindly amusement. She was so transparent! Her shocked disapproval of the intimacy obtaining between her former charge and Mr. Develyn, her discreet but avid interest in the gentleman's personality, her sentimental hunger for some hint of romance, all had been plain for the discerning eye to read. And where Armi was concerned, Francesca's eye had been trained to discernment from childhood. She had been at considerable pains to throw dust in the eyes of her kind preceptress but the exercise had caused her to search her own heart and she was dismayed at what she found there.

Could it be that after all these years of determined spinsterhood she had indeed formed a tendre for Robert Develyn? Honesty compelled her to admit that she had never felt this weakness—for such she considered it—for any other man. There had been admirers enough. Some professed to have fallen in love with her voice, others with her unusual personality—and all of them, she had thought cynically, were undoubtedly attracted by her handsome fortune. She had flirted light-heartedly with two or three but the game soon palled. And she had no desire at all to flirt with Robert. She simply enjoyed his society, matching her wits against his, listening to his plans, advising, arguing, laughing with him. It was so *comfortable*! But surely that did not mean that she was in love with him?

Yet all day long she had been aware of a sinking of her spirits. She had ascribed it to the ending of her holiday, for tomorrow, though no definite arrangements had been made, she assumed that they would start for home; had chided herself for childishness, for just so had she felt as a child when her birthday or Christmas was over for another whole, long year. She could not be, she *would* not be in love. She had done with that folly years ago.

And what of Robert? She would be a fool not to recognise that he took pleasure in her company. Even if pity had been his primary motive in planning her inclusion in this London jaunt, she was prepared to swear that he had enjoyed their evenings together every bit as much as she had.

She settled down in the corner of the chaise, turned her back on the scenery, and contemplated the future. It seemed to offer a continuation of their friendship along its present lines. They might ride together more often now that hunting was done; perhaps he would offer to escort her to lectures or concerts in Tunbridge Wells—that sort of thing. Surely a pleasant prospect? Far better than she had dreamed of six months ago. She found it positively depressing.

Very well. Then what *did* she want?

The late Earl of Finmore had loathed hypocrisy above all other weakness. "Be as selfish, as ruthless as you choose," he had once said to Francesca. "But don't be a hypocrite. Never pretend that your motives are pure and disinterested when a moment's rational consideration would show you very plainly that they were not. Be a sinner if you must—but be an honest one."

Curled in the corner of a chaise descending High-gate Hill she shut her eyes tightly and tried to follow his lordship's advice. What *did* she really want?

A picture of Robert Develyn's lean, bronzed face rose before her. Out of doors in all weathers he had never lost the deep tan that he had acquired in his wanderings. Against it the grey eyes looked cold, fathomless as lake water. Nose and jaw were forceful, even arrogant, and the lines about the mobile lips were bitter. Yet there was warmth and deep tenderness in him, she was convinced.

One hand crept up to her throat in a strange fright-ened little gesture like that of a lost child. She knew, now, what it was that she wanted. It was to feel those strong arms holding her close; hear the cool sardonic voice telling her that she was his and that he would never let her go; feel the fierce demanding pressure of his mouth on hers. How gladly, proudly, she would give herself to him; how joyously, together, they might forget the bitter wasted years.

For a brief space she drifted blissfully in her make-believe. Then she sighed and opened her eyes. Reality was a very different pair of shoes. She could see no hope of attaining her heart's desire. Robert was not in the least in love with her—else he had surely betrayed it this past week. As it was, though he had sometimes viewed her approvingly, perhaps even admiringly, there had been no hint of any warmer feeling. He might take her arm for guidance or support, always to release it promptly the moment the need was past. There had been no charming compliments, no eloquent glances, no lingering hand-clasps.

Thus Francesca—well versed in the ways of light flirtation if not in those of love. She had, however, the grace to acknowledge that, even had he desired her, he was not the kind of man to offer her a *carte blanche*. He was too fastidious. With him it would be marriage or nothing.

Marriage, then? What was there to prompt him to marriage—with anyone, least of all herself? He had a motherless daughter to rear and a large household to run. But anyone could see that he and Robin were getting along very comfortably as they were. And any way, who wanted to be married on those terms—just for usefulness and convenience?

The shade of Lord Finmore said, "My girl, you know very well you'd take him on any terms—and make what you could of it afterwards. I wouldn't put it past you to accept a *carte blanche* from him if he offered you one. And I'm not saying you'd be wrong at that. He's the man for you and you know it."

"If he did decide to marry again," replied Francesca with dignity, "he would scarcely choose a middle aged spinster with a smirched reputation. He may take his pick of all the eligible maidens on the marriage mart. Since he is already a wealthy man, considerations of fortune will not weigh with him. And if he looks to ally himself with noble birth he will not look at Francesca Thornish."

The shade threw up metaphorical hands in despair at such a poor-spirited attitude in one who had been taught to depend upon her own resources, and departed. Francesca finished her journey in planning a variety of distractions that might enable her to forget this sudden madness which had possessed her. Since all of them involved leaving South Gates, she soon found that they were of little use. Italy? Well—she could not, in any case, go there until after Armi's visit in June, and then it would be insufferably hot. The Lake District, then? It would be cool and fresh enough in those wild hills. Yes. And there would be far too much time for reflection and loneliness. In fact, it soon became apparent that, whatever her sufferings, Miss Thornish had no present intention of removing from South Gates. Not, at any rate, while Mr. Develyn remained unwed.

The immediate future assumed a brighter aspect when, upon her return, she was told that a package and a letter had been delivered during her absence. Both were from Mr. Develyn. The letter was brief and to the point. He had sent her some books which might help to beguile a solitary evening. The rather battered copy of Belzoni's 'Narrative of the Operations and Recent Discoveries within the Pyramids, Temples and

Tombs and Excavations in Egypt and Nubia' was his own, and he had thought she might like to dip into it. He hoped she would accept the other two as a small gift to mark the occasion. Scott's 'The Antiquary' had seemed to him an irresistible title, and though he had not read it himself the bookseller had assured him that it was Sir Walter's own favourite. And just in case she was heartily sick of the whole breed of antiquaries and all their works, which was, alas! only too probable, he had added 'Hyperion and Other Poems'.

A second paragraph—the writing sprawling a little now, in his haste, bade her think of him in his ordeal, and then asked permission to join her for breakfast next day so that he could tell her all about it and they could discuss the arrangements for their return.

Francesca's spirits soared. To have found time to think of her, to write to her, on *such* a day, argued a degree of regard far greater than she had dared to count upon. Even the fact that he seemed to be in haste to return to Saxondene could not quell the new spring of hope within her. For a confirmed spinster rapidly approaching middle age she spent her solitary evening in a perfectly ridiculous fashion. After an early dinner she retired to her room to pore over her new treasures in the sympathetic candle light. The letter must be read and re-read with careful attention to the style and character of the writing. The books must be examined and fondled, and her name and the date, which were inscribed in two of them, carefully compared with the writing in the letter. The ink looked different, so she decided that he had bought them some time previously—and delighted in the thought. She paid most attention to the Belzoni book because it was

Robert's own and, by its appearance, well read. But a glance at its pages made her shudder as she wondered if Robert, too, had run such risks, undergone such horrifying experiences. After that she contented herself with holding the volume lovingly against her cheek because his hands had touched it.

Presently she began to wander restlessly about the room, setting the appointments of her dressing table to rights, studying her reflection in the mirror, trying to decide which dress she would wear for breakfast next day. Perhaps it would be wisest to put on her travelling dress in case he was anxious to make an early start. But surely there would be time to change while Anna finished her packing, and the travelling dress, though neat and workmanlike, was rather masculine in style, whereas at the moment she was feeling particularly feminine.

Careful study of her wardrobe decided her to wear a simple but charming gown of blond. It was really an afternoon dress, but since it was so very plainly made she did not think a mere male would recognise that. The high neck was finished with a tiny ruff of its own fabric and a matching ruffle edged the full skirt. But the tightly fitted bodice and tiny waist were calculated to emphasize a charming figure, and the natural creamy tone of the unbleached silk was very becoming to her colouring.

That problem settled, she turned to finger the stuff of the golden ball dress, half wondering what had possessed her to buy such an extravagant thing, yet still wishing with passionate earnestness that by some chance Robert might see her wearing it. Sadly she recalled that his wife had been petite and fair, ethereally lovely. It seemed improbable that he should take a fancy for a great tall maypole of a girl—even in a golden gown. Her lips closed in a firm line. At least she would try. He liked her. That was a good beginning.

Weary at last she climbed into bed and blew out the candle. Under her pillow was a well worn book, and it was with one hand still smoothing this unusual adjunct to a maiden's slumbers that she finally fell asleep.

Possible the shade of his late lordship looked down and grinned and nodded approval.

Nine

Francesca woke early next day but for one reason or another her toilet seemed to take longer than usual. So she was a little late for breakfast. Mr. Develyn had already arrived and was standing by the window with his back to her glancing at a newspaper. She had good cause to be grateful for this since at the mere sight of him she felt a scalding rush of colour suffuse her cheeks. *That* was what came of day-dreaming about the man, she thought crossly, and walked over to the window very slowly, hoping that her agitation was not apparent.

Fortunately Mr. Develyn was in a slight difficulty of his own. On his way to his breakfast engagement he had chanced upon a street flower seller and, feeling relaxed and happy after the tensions of the previous night, had impulsively bought a posy of sweet violets for Francesca. It had then seemed to him that everyone he met stared at him in mild surprise until he began to feel as though he was carrying an oversize bouquet. He almost tossed the thing into the gutter but a certain native obstinacy prevented him. What he had done he would hold by. He, too, had been thankful for a breathing space in which to compose a nonchalant phrase or two to accompany his floral offering.

So it was perhaps natural that both should hurry into speech and so speak together.

"To remind you that Spring—the real Spring, not this city counterfeit—is waiting for you at home," said Mr. Develyn, bowing.

"I am so sorry. Have I kept you waiting long? I did not think it was so late," apologised Miss Thornish.

Then they both stopped short, laughing, the awkward moment was over, and there was excuse and to spare for bright eyes and glowing cheeks. Francesca breathed a silent prayer of gratitude to the kindly guardian angel—female, she was convinced—who had caused her to choose the dress she was wearing. No colour could have been better designed to set off the violets. And Mr. Develyn, seeing her pleasure in the trivial gift, forgot his embarrassment and gave himself up to carefree enjoyment.

Neither the lady nor the gentleman accorded the excellent meal that was served to them the critical appreciation that was its due, though both, despite the lady's admittedly love-lorn condition, addressed it with good appetite. There was too much to talk about, too much to plan.

Mr. Develyn reported with becoming modesty that his talk had been, on the whole, well received. It presently emerged that he had already been approached to address the Society again. Possibly to give a series of talks, not only on his experiences in the field but on the methods used in deciphering hieroglyphic script.

"A very flattering suggestion," he admitted. "But I doubt if I am scholar enough to do justice to such a subject. I once had the privilege of meeting Champollion. What dedication! It taught me how feeble and amateurish were my own efforts. In any case I mustn't be boring on for ever about old, dead things on such a glorious morning. Tell me, are you in a vast hurry to return to South Gates, or do you agree that we have both earned a holiday?"

She was a little taken aback, having believed that *he* was the one who was in haste to be home again, and murmured something non-committal about the whole of her visit being a holiday.

"Because," he explained eagerly, "I wondered if you would care to drive out with me this morning. In fact I took the liberty of hiring a phaeton and procuring entrance tickets for Richmond Park in the hope of persuading you to accompany me. We could lunch in Richmond if you cared for it. But I scarcely know what to suggest for your entertainment this evening. Is there anything that you would particularly like to do? Now don't disappoint me by saying that you must go home today. You can't wish to be cooped up in a closed carriage in this glorious sunshine. To be driving in the Park will be much more to your taste."

"I shall like it above everything," she assured him, trying to moderate her delight in the invitation and to display only a seemly pleasure in the treat. "And there is no particular reason why I should go home today. As for tonight, I confess I am not in the mood for more play-going. I scarcely know what——" She stopped short. One finger went to her lip and she brooded thoughtfully for a moment. Then she looked up at him, head a little tilted, face brimming with mischief.

"May I really choose? And you will escort me to the entertainment of my choice?" she said demurely.

He eyed her warily, then laughed and accepted the challenge. "At your service, ma'am," he said with mock gallantry, and wondered what was coming.

"It so chances that there is a Masked Ball at the Opera House tonight," she told him, voice deliciously prim, eyes alight with laughter at the horror-stricken expression which met the announcement. "I would dearly love to attend this function and shall be very happy to accept of your escort."

"Francesca! You little wretch! You don't really mean it, do you? No, of course you don't. You can't."

"Yes I do. I told you how much I love to dance and so rarely have the opportunity."

"But I don't think you realise! These affairs are quite shockingly vulgar. No lady of standing would dream of appearing at one. You wouldn't like it at all."

Francesca might be deep in love with this censorious gentleman but she was unaccustomed to having her decisions disputed. There was also another reason for her desire to attend the ball, a reason which she did not propose to explain to him.

"I thought we were agreed that I was shameless past praying for," she reminded him. "Certainly I would never claim to be a 'lady of standing'." And then, more coaxingly, "Besides, I shall be masked. So who is to know? I do, truly, want to go."

There was a touch of wistful longing in face and voice that he could not deny. "Very well," he said ruefully. "It shall be as you wish. But I had best warn you that even in my heyday I was no dancing man. A waltz I might manage with reasonable credit and even the country dances if I am placed at the bottom of the set, but the intricacies of quadrille and cotillion were always beyond me."

She smiled, content to have gained her will. "I expect you under-rate yourself. But I shall be quite satisfied with a waltz or two. We can always sit and watch the performance of others, you know. I daresay it will be quite as amusing as some of the plays we have seen."

"I had best see if I can reserve a box before we set out for Richmond," decided Mr. Develyn. "That will afford us some measure of comfort and we shall at least be able to eat supper without being jostled by people whose notion of enjoyment is to drink too much before they embark on the perils of the dance floor. Can you be ready in, let us say, an hour's time? Put on a warm wrap," he added, studying her light gown critically. "There is quite a cool breeze in spite of the sunshine."

Chance decreed that he should be able to hire a box in the second tier. The patron who engaged it for the season had broken a leg in the hunting field and was unlikely to require it for several weeks. Mr. Develyn was doubtful if this unfortunate gentleman would ever see the guineas that he handed over for the doubtful privilege of using the box for one night, but that was no concern of his. He was not even sure if he was grateful for his good fortune. To be sure it was satisfactory to be able to gratify Miss Thornish's expressed wish, but if no box had been available, perhaps she would have yielded to wiser counsels and abandoned the whole project. In any event he did not propose to allow the prospect of a dreadful evening to cloud his pleasure in the projected excursion to Richmond. And when he saw Francesca's face of delight at his news he was brought to believe that the evening might not be so very bad after all.

Since both parties to it were in a mood for enjoyment, the visit to Richmond was a resounding success. The hired phaeton was, perhaps, a trifle shabby, but since Mr. Develyn was driving his own horses there was no cause for complaint on *that* head. Once the park was reached and he had taken the edge off the greys he suggested that Francesca might like to drive and was soon confirmed in his belief that she would be very much at home with the ribbons. Not that she attempted anything particularly dashing. She took her time in establishing a good understanding with her horses, drove them well up to their bits, feather-edged a sharpish turn rather neatly and imbued her passenger with a comfortable confidence. Mr. Develyn, who intensely disliked being driven and had never before allowed a female to handle his greys, relaxed his vigilance and permitted himself to enjoy the beauty of Richmond Park on as perfect a spring morning as any he could remember. Francesca, well aware that his watchful readiness to avert threatened disaster had been withdrawn, smiled a little and eased the greys to a gentle amble so that she, too, might enjoy the passing scene.

They lunched at the Star and Garter and sampled the famous cheese cakes named for Queen Caroline's maids of honour. Mr. Develyn, a punctilious host, spoke of the several places of interest to be seen in the town itself, but Francesca could not summon up any enthusiasm for observatories nor even for places where such famous people as Chaucer or Sir Joshua Reynolds had lived. At the moment she found Mr. Develyn more stimulating and absorbing than the mysteries of the planetary system, and, though he could neither write verse like Chaucer nor paint portraits like Sir Joshua, his warm human magnetism was infinitely to be preferred to the distant echoes of the footsteps of genius. So they spent the afternoon in strolling about the winding paths in the park, exclaiming occasionally over some shrub that was a glory of early blossom, admiring the magnificent view of the river, but, in the main, simply content to be in each other's society. By the time that they were dressing for the evening's entertainment, neither of them could have enumerated with confidence the topics that they had discussed, though they would have been unanimous in agreeing that they had passed a wholly delightful day.

At the last moment Francesca decided not to wear the topaz diadem. It added a touch of magnificence which was out of keeping with the occasion, and, indeed, with her mood, which was wholly feminine and yielding. Moreover it made her look even taller than she really was. She had Anna dress her hair very simply, drawn back loosely from a centre parting and coiled into twists fastened with Italian pins at either side of her throat. Surveying her image in the glass she was well pleased. It might not be a fashionable style but it was undoubtedly becoming.

So thought Mr. Develyn, calling at the appointed hour to collect his fair charge, his mood one of resignation mingled with some wonderment as to how he had been beguiled into consenting to be present at a form of entertainment that might easily end in a vulgar fracas. At the sight of the young golden goddess who rose to greet him, he blinked. Then, swept by irresistible impulse, took the hand extended to him in greeting and carried it to his lips, bowing deeply after the charming fashion of an earlier day. Francesca coloured deliciously at the homage and curtsied her thanks.

"Do you like m-my gown?" she asked shyly, stammering a little because almost she had said, "Do you like me?"

Mr. Develyn, recovering his aplomb, assured her that she looked charmingly. It was a pity, he added, that modern fashions did not permit him to match her in elegance. Only the brocaded coats, satin breeches and silk stockings of his grandfather's day could have hoped to vie with such a vision. Had he but been warned in time he might have been able to provide himself with an appropriate costume. She laughed at that and told him that he looked extremely distinguished in his evening dress; and that, considering the fuss that he had made over just *attending* the masquerade, she could well imagine his consternation had he been required to wear fancy dress as well. She then permitted him to hand her into the waiting hackney. There was then some delay since there seemed to be a slight dispute over the instructions that he was giving to the driver. However, it could not have been anything of consequence, since when he eventually joined her he was laughing.

"You may not have required my services to bail you out," he told Francesca when he had recovered his composure, "but you are plainly bent on wrecking my reputation as a man of sober and reliable habits. When I told this fellow to drive us to Covent Garden he gasped at me, and then suggested that I must be— in his phrase—'lushy.' I *did* succeed in convincing him that I was perfectly sober, whereupon he suggested that maybe I'd got the wrong day; that it wasn't the "hopera" tonight but the "meskeride" and *that* wasn't no place for respectable parties to be "a-goin' of". However, I managed to enlist his sympathies by explaining that it was the lady who was set upon the enterprise, so that he finally consented to convey us to our destination, though not without a final dark hint about " 'oping the lidy wosn't wearing no walliable joolery". It so chances that this is the same fellow who drove me about to my various engagements last night. Apparently he finds it difficult to reconcile my present activities with the company I kept then."

Francesca laughed with him, fully appreciating the bewilderment of a man who had marked his passenger as a scholar, respectable, erudite and dry as dust, and now found himself utterly confounded.

She said mischievously, "Your uncle was used to say that it was good for a man, at times, to be deprived of the usual trappings of his existence. *So* he would soon discover if he was still a man. That was when we were travelling in North Africa," she went on reminiscently. "He went incognito. Said that a parade of wealth and rank would only attract thieves and hangers-on." She chuckled. "*You* would not have approved, I fear. I wore boy's clothes and passed as his nephew because I could not endure to travel in a stuffy litter as poor Cathy did."

"My uncle was a brave man," retorted Robert. "Had

I been in his shoes I would have insisted on the litter. The thought of the possible consequences had your sex been discovered would have hardened my heart against your best persuasions."

"Well—he did make me promise that I would always carry my pistols," she admitted. And then, suddenly brave in the darkness of the cab, "What would you have done if I had defied your orders?"

"Tied you to the camel's back—or sold you to the first desert prince we met to be the pearl of his harem," he said, smiling. "And that is the kind of treatment you may expect tonight if you go counter to my wishes. Though I doubt if anyone lacking the wealth of an eastern potentate could find the price I should demand for my golden girl."

For once Francesca was silenced. She had never heard him in this vein before. It was sharply exhilarating—more exciting even than fencing with swords— and she was furious with herself that she had not the wit to devise a ready answer. While still she hesitated he went on, "Much as I deplore your addiction to masculine dress, I could almost wish that you were wearing it tonight. It would certainly simplify the task of ensuring that you are not subjected to insult or indignity. We could sit peacefully in our box, enjoy our supper, savour our wine, laugh at all the oddities, quiz all the pretty girls——"

"And you would not be required to dance with me," finished Francesca gently.

Above the gentle 'clop' of the horse's hoofs she distinctly heard his indrawn breath. Then he said quietly, "That is very true."

There was a queer, tense little silence. Then the

quiet voice went on, "Very well. I will renounce the easy company of my scrubby urchin for the privilege of dancing with the golden lady."

Since Francesca scarcely knew how to answer him, it was fortunate that at this point the cab stopped and the driver came round to suggest that they might prefer to alight here since there was such a press of vehicles immediately ahead that they would finish the journey much more quickly on foot. A glance out of the window confirming this view, Mr. Develyn bade Francesca put on her mask before they stepped out into the lights. She obeyed, and tied the strings of her domino so that it hid most of her glimmering gown. He helped her to alight and drew her arm firmly through his.

The crowds on the flag walk were good humoured enough but there was a good deal of pushing and jostling as they craned to get a better view. Francesca was very grateful for that strong protective arm and began to realise that Mr. Develyn had not overstated the case when he had described these masquerades as vulgar squeezes. She was thankful enough to reach the shelter of their box and to sit quietly for a while watching the gay throng disporting itself below them.

For anyone who loved colour and did not mind a good deal of noise it was an exhilarating sight. The Opera House itself offered a magnificent setting, though she could not help thinking that tonight, in the light of so many candles, the scarlet and white and gold of its hangings and decorations looked a trifle garish. She wondered a little that this had never struck her before when she had attended performances of the Italian opera. Perhaps it was the riot of colour on the dancing

floor that heightened the effect, for, to be sure, every
costume that one could imagine and a good many that
one would never have dreamed of, seemed to be presented on the crowded stage, hopping and twirling and
jigging in a shifting, dazzling kaleidoscope. She saw a
grim, black-clad headsman dancing with a nymph—
a nymph so diaphanously clothed that she made Francesca's boyish riding dress seem prudishly proper. It
was a pity that she could scarcely direct her escort's
attention to so shockingly immodest an exhibition.

She leaned her elbows on the ledge at the front of
the box and rested her chin on her clasped hands,
watching with fascinated eyes. Most of the women
were in costume, but quite a number of the men wore
ordinary evening dress. Many of them had not even
troubled to don mask or domino.

Mr. Develyn's voice spoke in her ear. "When these
country dances are finished, we are to have the Vien-
nese Waltz. At this stage of the evening it should be
possible to dance it in moderate comfort. Later, frankly,
it will be a mad romp. Will you honour me?"

Francesca shrank. In her seclusion of the box she
was enjoying herself but her confidence faltered at the
thought of joining the mêlée. Yet after all her bold
proclamations she could scarcely decline.

"Everyone else seems to be in costume," she hedged.
"I should look very much out of place."

Mr. Develyn laughed outright. "You *are* very much
out of place," he told her. "But if you imagine that
so feeble an excuse will serve you now, you are sadly
mistaken. I was promised my dances, if you remember,
and you cannot be so unkind as to disappoint me."

The voice was pleasant, the words were courteous.

But his face was alight with teasing triumphant laughter. He might just as well have said, "There! You see? Foolish child! Why could you not allow me to know what was best for you?" And in a sudden upsurge of rebellion she smiled brilliantly back at him and began to loosen the strings of her domino. "One cannot dance comfortably in these things," she explained sweetly. "So long as I am masked no one will recognise me. Listen! They are striking up for the waltz now."

Divided between amusement and admiration of her spirit, Mr. Develyn escorted her down the stairs and on to the dancing floor. It was ten years since he had last adventured so, but the lilt of the waltz is irresistible and after some initial stiffness and awkwardness they discovered that their steps suited very well. If there was nothing outstandingly graceful about their performance at least they enjoyed themselves very much and were quite reluctant to leave the floor when the sets for quadrilles began to form. Francesca did indeed look up at her partner hopefully, but he shook his head. "Perhaps another time," he apologised. "Not tonight. I cannot even recall the sequence of the figures. Besides—I don't suppose you ate much dinner. I know I didn't. We'll have supper now, and watch the fun. We might dance again later if it doesn't get too rough."

Francesca was not particularly hungry but a cool drink would be very acceptable. They passed an hour very pleasantly, toying with an excellent supper and sipping iced champagne cup while the stage below them grew more and more crowded and it became apparent that many of the dancers had partaken rather too freely of liquid refreshment. They were still debating whether or not it would be comfortable to dance again when a knock fell on the door of the box.

The man who stood in the doorway would have been noticeable in any company for his height and his arrogant bearing. Not all the effeminacy of silks and velvet, the laces and love-knots of his cavalier costume could conceal his dominant masculinity. He had doffed his plumed hat on entering the box and was now wrestling with the strings of his mask which had worked themselves into a knot. There was a gleam of white teeth in a charming smile beneath the mask as he said, "A shocking intrusion, I know. But when a man recognises a long-lost cousin I trust he may be forgiven for making himself known. How long is it, Robert? Fifteen years?"

At this point he lost patience with the mask strings and snapped them, revealing a handsome countenance lit by a pair of merry blue eyes. Eyes of so dark a blue, shaded by such long and curling lashes that Francesca could not help feeling they were wasted on a mere man. She had noticed the dashing Cavalier once or twice among the dancers. He was one of a party of six who occupied a ground floor box on the opposite side from theirs, and apart from his striking appearance he was an excellent dancer. In view of his remarks it scarcely needed Robert's, "Wilfred! Good God! What on earth are you doing in this galère?" to advise her that she was in the presence of the new Earl of Finmore.

"Oh! I'm with a party of friends," said the newcomer insouciantly. "Town is so deuced flat at the moment—one must do *something* to put the time along —and someone suggested that these masquerades were quite amusing. If it comes to that, cousin, I might ask the same question of you—if it were not that your reason for being here is easy to see." And he sketched a slight bow in Francesca's direction.

It was the kind of arch remark that set Francesca's teeth on edge and scarcely what one expected of a well-bred gentleman and it was said with such confident charm that it was impossible to resent it. In any case there was no time to do so, for the Earl, now gravely courteous, was asking if he might not be presented to the lady.

"But of course," he said thoughtfully, the introduction duly made. "Uncle Miles's protégée. I have heard so much in your praise, ma'am, but I see I was not told the half."

Francesca thought the gentleman stood in need of a sharp set-down. This was just the sort of cheap gallantry that she most disliked. But she could scarcely treat her host's cousin with the chilly civility that he deserved. She curtsied her acknowledgements and favoured Lord Finmore with a glance of tolerant amusement before raising her fan to hide her expression.

But this casual reception only spurred him to renewed efforts. "I looked to see you again on the dancing floor," he explained. "I missed you after the waltzes. Hoped to bespeak Miss Thornish's hand for the cotillion—with your permission, of course, Robert, but if I remember aright you were never a dancing man. You *will* do me the honour, won't you ma-am?"

Much as she loved dancing Francesca would have preferred to decline. It seemed to her discourteous to abandon Robert when he had brought her to the masquerade quite against his own wishes. Nor did she

at all care for his lordship's unblushingly piratical
approach. He seemed to her very much one of Fortune's spoiled darlings, expecting anything that he
fancied to drop into his lap just for the asking. But
Robert, sensing her hesitation, and guessing in part its
cause, made it impossible for her to refuse without
downright rudeness by saying pleasantly, "You will
enjoy that, won't you? You will do very much better
with Wilfred than with me. And I shall enjoy watching you."

That was not strictly true, he thought ruefully, watching them take their places in the set. A cotillion, well
danced, was a pretty thing to be sure. But the sight of
Francesca dancing it with his cousin Wilfred, smiling
up at him, apparently coquetting with him as the
character of the dance demanded, gave him no pleasure at all. There could be no denying that they made
a very striking pair. Even in that motley assembly a
number of heads were turning to watch them. And
though Francesca was still masked, Wilfred was not.
Robert was not fully conversant with the details of his
cousin's recent career, but he knew enough to realise
that any lady who was singled out for particular attention by the gallant earl would probably become the
subject of scandalous conjecture. Why the deuce had
he suggested that she should dance? She would willingly
have foregone the pleasure, he knew. Pride had driven
him, as so often before in his boyhood encounters with
Wilfred. Fool that he was! He scanned the company
in the boxes anxiously, taking what comfort he could
from the belief that no female of any consequence
would dream of being present at such a rout, and
thankful to see Francesca shake her head decisively

at the end of the cotillion as she declined to dance again.

They came back to the box, Wilfred protesting that the night was yet young and that it was absurd to speak of leaving just when things were beginning to liven up. Francesca was firm. She was warm and thirsty and she would like another glass of that delicious cold drink, but then she would like to go home. It had been a full day and they meant to be off betimes next morning. Wilfred's air of disappointment at this decision was comical. Had she been seventeen, thought Francesca amusedly, she would quite have believed him to be seriously impressed with her charms. He began to speak nostalgically of the one holiday that he had spent at Saxondene in his boyhood, expressing himself with such fervent appreciation that Robert could not do other than throw out a casual suggestion that he must pay another visit to the place some day. This extremely vague invitation was seized upon with delight. Wilfred had engagements in Town for the next two days but he was practically free for the following week. Certainly there was nothing he could not defer. If Robert really meant it, then his cousin would certainly journey into Kent and they would spend a few days in recapturing boyhood's memories.

Robert raised a sardonic eyebrow at that. If *his* memory served him aright, the holiday in question had lasted for less than a week and was chiefly remarkable for the number of times that the pair of them had come to fisticuffs. Even Wilfred seemed to feel that he had slightly overdone the sentimental approach and added hastily that he had been meaning to visit Saxondene in any case. There were one or two business matters that he would like to discuss with Robert, and so much more comfortable to do so at leisure and see something of the charming Kentish countryside at the same time. From the sneaking glance that he directed at Miss Thornish no one was left in any doubt that she ranked high among the beauties of nature.

He took himself off at last, making Francesca a perfectly splendid bow, plumed hat swept across his breast. In a spirit of pure michief she played up to him, extending her hand for his kiss, which encouraged him to bestow upon her the full eloquence of his gaze as well. She was hard put to it not to giggle—until she saw the thunderous expression on Mr. Develyn's brow which swiftly dispelled any such impulse.

In contrast to the gay banter that they had exchanged during their drive to the Opera House, the return journey was a silent one. Mr. Develyn spoke only to enquire if Francesca was perfectly comfortable and sufficiently warm, and then, after a brooding pause, to arrange the time at which he should take her up next day. Thanks to an excellent education in the moods of men, the lady very wisely suppressed her own eagerness to discuss the evening's entertainment in every detail, confining her remarks to an expression of gratitude for a perfectly delightful day, and meekly promising to be ready to set out in good time on the morrow.

Ten

Francesca was ashamed to acknowledge it, but after the excitements of her stay in Town she found the hum-drum routine of South Gates very dull. There was plenty to be done. Her garden, which was a great delight to her, was clamouring for attention. Merlin, who would not yet suffer anyone else to bestride him, was urgently in need of hard steady exercise, and she was planning the redecoration of the Hornbys' sitting room. But none of these activities sufficed to drive out her thoughts of Robert Develyn, her longing for his physical presence. And for three days she did not so much as set eyes upon him. Robin came and went as usual but she could not question the child as to her father's whereabouts.

She grew short-tempered and irritable, reaching the point at which she longed to snap at dear, kind Cathy Hornby who would persist in questioning her about London, wanting to know the details of all the latest fashions, which prominent personages she had chanced to see at the theatre, how the streets appeared with this new-fangled gas lighting and a dozen similar innocent topics.

Exercising Merlin was the best way of assuaging her miserable restlessness but unfortunately it also raised another problem. What was she to do with him? He was maturing splendidly, even better than she and the Earl had dreamed when they had planned for him a glorious career on the race course before he was retired to stud. But not even Francesca could envisage a female managing that career. And who could she trust to do it for her? One name, of course, sprang immediately to mind—the very name that she was trying so hard to drive from her thoughts.

She would have been vastly comforted could she have taken a clairvoyant peep into Mr. Develyn's state of mind. That gentleman had been considerably shocked by his own reaction to Wilfred's intervention at the masquerade. Until that moment he had not realised how completely he had come to regard Miss Thornish as his own particular property. They had known each other scarcely six months and their intimacy had grown so quietly, so naturally, that not till he saw her walk away from him on Wilfred's arm did he awake to a totally changed situation.

The antagonism of their first encounter was now only food for occasional teasing. The critical appraisal of those early days, his shocked disapproval of Miss Thornish's freedom of speech and manners and of her predilection for wearing masculine dress when it seemed to her better suited to the activity of the moment, had melted entirely. He still preferred to see her in her softer, feminine guise, but she wore her boy's clothes so unaffectedly that he had come to take them as much for granted as she did. They had fallen into the habit of easy companionship over the fencing lessons and Robin's music, but it was not until the week that they had spent in London that he had awakened to the realisation of how much he had come to depend on that companionship. Wilfred's swift appropriation of the lady had left him furiously but helplessly indignant.

Just because she had so freely given him of her time and her company did not entitle him to sole possession of her interest. She was perfectly free to bestow the pleasure of her company where she wished. But he hoped she would not choose to bestow very much of it upon Wilfred. What possessed the fellow that he must come to Saxondene at this damned inconvenient juncture of affairs? Just precisely why it was inconvenient, Mr. Develyn did not attempt to explain to himself. He thought instead about his cousin Wilfred and the motives that might be actuating that gentleman. What did he hope to gain? Robert was prepared to swear that they liked each other no better than they had done in their schooldays so why this sudden desire for his society? Perhaps the animosity between two schoolboys had been born of jealousy. Wilfred—at Eton, as family tradition demanded—had looked down his nose at a mere Harrovian, and the Harrovian had been at some pains to demonstrate equality if not superiority in the sporting field. Since that time their paths had met but rarely. Robert's knowledge of his cousin was only what all the world knew—that since his succession to the title he was one of the most eligible bachelors in Town. A reputation for libertinism and rumours of

extravagance in the maintenance of his racing stable
were unlikely to deter the match-making mamas, with
the lure of the Finmore fortune to encourage them,
while his handsome face and figure and the practised
charm of his manner might be expected to wreak
havoc in any maiden heart. So that the heart was not
Francesca Thornish's, Robert did not greatly care.

Into this atmosphere of uncertainty came Wilfred,
Earl of Finmore, to prove himself the pleasantest,
the easiest of guests. He had brought his valet with
him, hoping that this imposition would not too greatly
incommode his host, but insisted on stabling his horses
in the village and quartering his groom and coachman
at the inn. He was pleased with everything but dis-
criminatingly so, seasoning his approval with an occasional suggestion for possible improvement. His
interest in the working of the estate seemed perfectly
sincere. It was certainly creditable in one whose vast
holdings made Saxondene appear little more than a
tidy manor.

In the social aspect he was equally at home. Robert
gave a bachelor dinner party for him, a quiet affair,
since most of the younger, gayer sparks had already
departed for Town. Wilfred did not appear to exert
himself, yet somehow seemed to have the happy knack
of showing up the other guests at their most entertaining. Sir Lucas made the general approval plain when
he told Finmore gruffly that it was a sad pity he must
choose to live in such an outlandish part of the world.
They could show him some very pretty hunting country if he cared to spend a season in Kent.

Francesca, too, gave a dinner party for the cousins,
inviting the Rector and his wife who, with Mrs. Hornby,

made up her table. Save for the small numbers which made general conversation a necessity it was a surprisingly formal party for that friendly, homely house, thought Robert. Francesca was unusually quiet, dignified and serene in her dark green gown, attentive to the comfort of her guests but in subdued mood. With Wilfred on her right hand and the Rector on her left she divided her attention impartially, taking her share of the conversational burden with practised ease but initiating no topics other than those of general interest. Wilfred was superb. The salty anecdotes of the bachelor party might never have soiled his lips. He delighted the two older ladies with a detailed description of the young Princess Victoria of Kent whom he had chanced to see some years previously at Kensington Palace, the happiest theme he could have chosen, since Mrs. Whittingham was able to cap it with a story of her own of seeing the royal child riding her donkey in Jordan Place during one of her frequent sojourns in Tunbridge Wells. The ladies were encouraged to tell him of their fluttering forebodings on the oddity of having some day to accept a queen as their ruling monarch. Not since the reign of Queen Anne, they assured him solemnly, had such a thing befallen. Mrs. Whittingham, greatly daring, even ventured the opinion that a queen would certainly require the guidance of a good and wise husband in the discharge of her onerous duties, after which she and Mrs. Hornby settled happily to the task of selecting possible candidates for the position. Lord Finmore nodded, drew a sober mouth, agreed with their sage pronouncements and won the esteem of both ladies by his deferential attitude. Neither of them would ever have been brought to believe that he had scarcely heard one word in three.

The gentlemen did not linger very long over their wine, excellent though it was, before joining the ladies in the drawing room. Two card tables had been set up, candles arranged to give light to the players and fresh packs of cards laid out invitingly. But before Francesca could suggest their use Wilfred intervened.

"Will you not sing for us, Miss Thornish?" he begged winningly. "My uncle was used to say that you might have made a career for yourself as a professional singer had you been born into a different walk of life. I know how highly he esteemed your talents, and he was a noted connoisseur."

If there was a hint of 'double entendre' in the remark about the lady's talents, a salacious gleam in the handsome blue eyes, these were masked by the charming urgency of the voice. Lord Finmore, in beguiling mood, would be difficult to resist. His plea was promptly endorsed by the Rector.

"Yes, indeed!" he exclaimed. "It is by far too long since I heard you sing—except in church, of course."

Francesca suspected that Cathy and Mrs. Whittingham would much prefer to play cards but it was difficult to refuse when two of her guests were so pressing.

She settled herself quietly at the piano, declining all offers of accompaniment or assistance with turning of music. She preferred to accompany herself, she explained, and since she meant to sing only one or two simple songs would manage the accompaniments from memory. She sat for a moment, head bent in thought, then straightened to smile across at the Rector.

"Under the greenwood tree?" she queried. "It was

used to be a favourite with you." And without more ado began to sing.

To her familiar friends the magic of her voice came as no surprise. They listened comfortably, Mrs. Hornby going so far as to glance complacently at the card tables and to reflect that two short songs would not long delay the serious business of the evening.

On the two younger gentlemen the beautiful voice had a different effect. It was so much a social practice to lavish fulsome praise on young ladies who displayed some modest musical talent that Wilfred had automatically composed his face into the expression of polite appreciation that he reserved for such occasions. As the first round, beautiful notes fell upon his ear, it changed to a startled, intent, listening look. Good God! Such a voice was worth a fortune! The wench was quite passable looking, too, and with the aid of stage makeup ——. Why the devil was she mouldering away in this benighted spot when she must know that wealth and fame could be hers for the taking? Even the old scandal that connected her name with his uncle's could be turned to good account in a stage career. And she had no reputation to lose, so what was stopping her?

Wilfred had been considerably startled to find the Rector and his wife dining at the home of one whom he regarded as little better than a high class courtesan. For there could be no question about that. First there had been Hugh O'Malley and then his uncle. And now it looked as though Cousin Robert had inherited the lady's favours along with the Saxondene estate. Very cosy the pair of them had looked in that snug little box at the masquerade. He could only assume that the kindly cleric was ignorant of the shadier details of Miss Thornish's career.

> "Who doth ambition shun,
>   And loves to live i' the sun,"

sang the clear voice, almost as if explaining the girl's odd behaviour. He glanced across at his cousin. But after the initial shock, Robert had himself well in hand. His countenance betrayed no more than the absorption of a rapt listener. Odd creatures, women, mused Wilfred. Imagine a passionate vital piece like this one— the man of the world could read the physical signs well enough—devoting the best years of her life to an old man, and now to his dried-up stick of a cousin! And tossing aside the golden opportunities that her talents could have brought her. Why! He wouldn't have minded having a touch at her himself! At least it would have served to alleviate the intolerable boredom of this deadly dull visit. But if he hoped to come to terms with Robert, best do nothing to alienate him. He wondered how much longer he must spend in establishing himself as the affectionate cousin, the thoroughly sound country bumpkin, before he ventured to broach the real purpose of his visit. And so far he had not so much as set eyes on his quarry. Where the devil had they hidden him?

The appreciative veneer masking his thoughts once more, Wilfred stopped listening.

Robert had settled himself for the music in a mood of some annoyance. Why had not *he* thought to ask Francesca to sing? From scraps of information that she had let fall he knew perfectly well that she must have

a considerable gift. Uncle Miles was not such a fool
as to have taken her to Italy to ensure first-rate tuition
for her had it been otherwise. To be sure, they had
rarely met in the evenings so perhaps his omission was
natural enough, but it was still annoying that it had
been Wilfred, and Wilfred at his most charming, who
had repaired it. The fellow might have improved somewhat since his school days but he was too damned
smooth by half.

At the first golden phrase his irritability died. It was
an incredible voice, smooth, almost sexless, more like
a boyish treble than a woman's voice, and it poured
out as effortlessly as bird song. There was no affecta-
tion of pose, no vocal flourishes. Francesca simply
opened her throat and sang. Robert was not particularly
musical but it brought to his mind a phrase he had
picked up somewhere. *'Bel canto.'* That was it. And
it was magical in effect. He wanted it to go on and on.

The little phrase at the end of the first song found
him silent. He did not join in the polite patter of ap-
plause, simply waited impatiently for the singer to
continue. She played a few desultory phrases, as though
choosing thoughtfully among her repertoire and then
began to sing 'Where e'er you walk' to Handel's beautiful setting from Semele. And now the choirboy voice
was muted and tender and indisputably feminine. As
though the last veil had been torn from his eyes Robert
was suddenly aware of the sweetness and the loyalty,
the capacity for loving that were as much a part of the
singer as the impudent boyish swagger that guarded
the vulnerable heart. In that moment he knew beyond
all doubting that he wanted Francesca Thornish as
he had never wanted a woman before. The youthful

passion that he poured out upon his first wife had not survived to mature. Shaken by her inability to respond, shattered by her infidelity, it had died painfully but inevitably. And the urgent need that clamoured now in mind and heart and body was as little like that youthful adoration as a hurricane is like a summer zephyr.

Living self-contained and at peace for years, Robert had thought himself long past falling a prey to the turmoil of emotions that now possessed him. It was a fortunate circumstance that he had lived much in countries where the maintenance of an impassive demeanour was essential to the conduct of any negotiation. That training helped him now. For however startling the revelation that had been vouchsafed him, however fierce his determination to win Francesca for his wife in the teeth of all opposition, he could scarcely propose marriage in the middle of a private party, even if one or two of those present would be concerned with the business of achieving it.

Quietly he added his thanks to the others' and expressed his pleasure in her singing. Wilfred was begging her to sing again, with an ingenuous eagerness and a play of fine eyes that Robert noted with suddenly sharpened dislike. The manner would have beseemed a much younger man—and Wilfred six months older than Robert himself!

But Francesca refused, pleasantly but definitely. The Rector and Mrs. Whittingham, she said lightly, had only accepted her invitation on the express understanding that cards, and not music, were to provide the evening's entertainment. And though the Rector protested vigorously at this slanderous statement it was plain from Mrs. Whittingham's expression that she, at any rate, endorsed Francesca's account of the matter.

Some discussion followed as to what they should play. Six was rather an awkward number, admitted the hostess, since they were all a litle past the age of enjoying round games. She had hoped that if four of her guests should elect to play whist, the fifth would be willing to play piquet or cribbage with her. She was, she confessed, a very indifferent whist player. A cut of the cards between the three gentlemen could decide who should be her victim she added, with a hint of the mischief that seemed so much more natural to her than the quiet dignity of her previous bearing.

The whim of the cards left Wilfred out of the first rubber of whist and he elected to play piquet rather than cribbage. A fine card player in his own circles he found scant entertainment in any game played for the chicken stakes favoured by the present company and took his place at the smaller table with resignation rather than elation at the prospect of having his hostess to himself for a little while.

On Robert the arrangement reacted differently. Because the repeated declarations of the piquet players might disrupt the solemn concentration essential to whist, the smaller table had been set at a little distance. The effect was to give it an air of seclusion, almost of intimacy. To Robert, gloomily watching the two animated faces in the intervals of his own play, Francesca and his cousin seemed to be getting on very well together. It occurred to him that his new-found love must be desirable in other eyes than his. It was probably only the fact that she had lived so strange and so secluded a life that had kept her so long a spinster.

And who could blame her if she took a fancy to becoming a countess when the new Earl of Finmore was so pleasant and popular a fellow and so obviously taken with her? He absent-mindedly discarded his last diamond, cleared trumps and led a small spade. His partner, Mrs. Whittingham, who had indicated strength in diamonds, stared at it disbelievingly. They lost the game and the rubber. Mrs. Whittingham wondered who had spread the word that Mr. Develyn was a good whist player. She was thankful to cut her husband as partner for the next rubber, the piquet players cheerfully proclaiming that the contest between *them* was far too close to permit any change of game at this stage.

Time slipped away. Wilfred fitted into the life of Saxondene as easily and comfortably as though he had no intention of ever removing. A careless remark brought out the story of the fencing lessons and he begged admission to what he insisted upon calling the *"salle d'armes"*. Like his uncle he was an exponent of the Italian school and no mean performer, but he accepted defeat at Robert's hands with easy good humour. He was no longer a conceited stripling who could never bear to be bested. Not, at any rate, when his aim was to please. Franesca, privileged to watch the encounter, glowed with primitive satisfaction that she had difficulty in dissembling.

The business that had brought Wilfred to Saxondene was never mentioned. It is difficult for a host to ask outright why a guest has practically invited himself to stay, and still more difficult to suggest that he declare his business, settle it, and go. On the one occasion when Robert managed to approach the subject he was told a somewhat evasive tale about his late lordship's diaries. Wilfred had entertained some thought of publishing them since they might be of interest to travellers and archaeologists. But since they were pretty liberally seasoned with pungent comments on prominent persons, he wondered if his cousin would care to glance through them first, give an opinion on their usefulness and make suggestions as to how far they should be edited.

While secretly admitting to an interest in the diaries, especially those which covered the years since the advent of Francesca Thornish into his lordship's life, Robert thought it a pretty feeble excuse for a visit which had already extended into its third week. If that was the only reason that had brought his cousin into Kent, he must be all about in his head. It could have been settled quite easily without his ever leaving Town.

He had to wait several more days before the true reason for the visitation emerged. He and Wilfred rode out early one morning to call upon Mr. Gilbey. That gentleman had for sale a half-brother of Hopover's, and Wilfred, who had taken a fancy to Hopover, was interested in trying him. But the call was never made, for as they were cantering gently along a grassy ride they were suddenly favoured with an excellent view of Francesca Thornish on the black stallion, Merlin.

Schooling was over for the morning and the pair were trotting back towards the small hedge-girt pasture that was Merlin's summer domain. At sight of them Wilfred reined in sharply and sat at gaze, his eyes narrowed to assess the quality of the animal he had come so far to find. Then he said slowly, "No wonder you kept him close hidden. But it's no good, you know.

That fellow belongs in the Finmore stud. I want him back." And then, more sharply, "Who's the lad you've put up on him? Seems to know his job. Good hands— and a light-weight, too. But can he ride a race? A jockey who's on good terms with his mount is half way to the winning post, but he'll need to be up to all the tricks of the trade before I'll take him on."

Eleven

His suavity for once a little ruffled by the error into
which he had fallen, Wilfred handled the business
badly from the start. Who would ever have dreamed
that the old man would have given a thoroughbred
stallion to a mere chit of a girl? Still less that he would
have gone to the pains of having the transaction legally
recorded. When first he had been told of the colt's
existence, Wilfred had naturally assumed that Robert
had taken him over along with the rest of the Saxondene stable—might even be unaware of his value. His
first reaction on learning the true situation was one
of satisfaction. A woman would be much easier to
manage. What use was the colt to her? It was just a
matter of price—and no need to pay too high at that.
But it was a sad pity that he had not known the true
facts sooner. If he had really put himself about, the
wench would have been eating out of his hand by now.
However it was not too late. A little address, a few

easy compliments, and the thing was done.

A little surprised to receive a request for a private interview from the gentleman, Francesca was on her guard from the outset. Whatever the Earl wanted with her, it would be something to *his* advantage rather than hers, she thought cynically. She liked him no better than she had done at their first meeting though his blatant confidence in the potency of his personal charm afforded her considerable amusement. She listened with critical appreciation to the smooth phrases in which he thanked her for receiving him and thought once again that he would be vastly improved by a few crushing set-downs. *If* it was possible for any imaginable snub to depress such an inflated conceit!

He went on to speak of having seen her riding Merlin that morning. His compliments on her superb management of a difficult mount were received with polite reserve, but his praise for the colt won a warmer response. Where horses were concerned Wilfred was genuine enough, even if quite unscrupulous. They were his one true passion and he knew by heart the breeding, the weaknesses, the racing records and current form, not only of all his own horses but those of all their likely rivals. Francesca could not but enjoy discussing Merlin with such an enthusiast.

When, however, he turned the talk to her plans for Merlin's future, she sensed danger. His manner was too sympathetic. He wondered a little, he explained, why his uncle should have burdened her with such a responsibility.

If he had said outright that it was unfair to so fine a colt to leave the management of his racing career to a woman, she would probably have agreed with him.

But the implied criticism of his uncle was just the thing to set up all her prickles.

"Merlin was given to me because it was I who planned the linking of those particular blood lines," she said, with deceptive gentleness. "His lordship had intended to repeat the mating that produced Jeronimo. It was at my suggestion that he decided rather to try what Magician could sire out of Merry Maid. When the foal showed promise he was delighted. Merlin was deeded to me as a yearling," she finished, a hint of warning in the careful use of the legal phrase.

The Earl ignored it. He was not particularly sensitive to overtones at any time and in this case he was bent only on achieving his set purpose.

"He should never have been taken out of Finmore," he said resentfully. "A proportion of his winnings and of the profits from his services might have been allowable. I would consider such an arrangement myself though I would prefer to buy outright. But back to Finmore he must go. Giving him away in the first case —the best colt of this decade—was an act of criminal folly."

Francesca heard him out in dignified silence, then rose, as an indication that the interview was now over. "Merlin is not for sale on any terms," she said quietly.

The Earl scowled up at her, making no attempt to rise but, instead, throwing himself back in his chair, hands thrust deep in his pockets and long legs sprawled out in an attitude that was in itself an insult in the presence of a lady.

"Think you've the whip hand, don't you?" he said unpleasantly. "Very well, then, name your price. But bear in mind I'm not the high-nosed fool my uncle was. You'll not chouse *me* out of a fortune."

Francesca's brows lifted in faint surprise. "I thought I had made it sufficiently plain," she said coldly. "Merlin is not for sale. You waste your time, my lord. And since I have a good deal to do, I will bid you good afternoon," and on the words she turned to ring for the maid to show him out.

Wilfred lost the last shreds of his temper. "Do you imagine that is the end of the matter?" he said between his teeth. "My uncle's hand is not over you now, you cheating doxy. *Him* you may have cozened with your fine airs and graces; and dear Cousin Robert is very fond, too, I perceive. But let him keep you never so close, I'll see to it that you rue this day's work. As for your precious Merlin—never think to see him win a race. He'll never have the chance. You'll wish you had taken my offer and kept him fit and able before I'm done with him."

Some odd lingering remnant of propriety gave him pause as Marian came in to answer the summons of the bell.

"His lordship is just leaving, Marian," said Francesca steadily. "When you have shown him out, will you please ask Mrs. Hornby to come to me."

The words of that vague but none the less terrifying threat hung uneasily in the air. She stood gazing out of the window, her eyes blind to the beauty of the garden over which she had toiled so patiently. Now that pride no longer required her to keep a brave face her mouth quivered piteously. Her hands were shaking, too, and cold despite the summer warmth. His lordship —her own beloved mentor—would have been ashamed of her, she reflected, and strove to assume the gallant bearing, the dauntless air that he would have demanded. But lacking the support of his physical presence it was not so easy and she was given scant time to master the betraying signs of her fears before the door opened once more and she returned, albeit reluctantly, to greet her chaperone.

But it was not dumpy, comfortable Catherine Hornby who stood on the threshold, but her husband; and in Francesca's present anxiety he still represented the comfort and security of the Earl's protection. She came to him eagerly, her whole expression brightening into relief and trust.

"Brand! How did you guess that 'twas you I needed? I meant only to ask Cathy if I could speak with you. I would not idly have disturbed your work."

He smiled down at her, enclosing the cold hands that she had held out to him in his warm, capable grasp. "I did not know. But Catherine has stepped down to the village to see some poor ailing body that sent for her. And Marian said you seemed a trifle out of frame when his lordship left. Has that under-bred pup been annoying you?"

The whole story came tumbling out then, and all her fears for Merlin's safety. He listened with frowning concentration, the very fact that he did not attempt to make light of her anxiety oddly comforting.

"He's an unpleasant piece, our Master Wilfred," he said reflectively, "for all his smooth seeming. I've known him these twenty years past and there's little I'd put past him." He mulled over the possibilities. "Not theft. Too easily traced, so 'twould do him no good. But maiming, now, I'd not rule out of court, so it could be done secretly."

His thoughtful look softened at Francesca's shocked gasp and frightened face. "Never fear, child. We'll not let it happen. But you must have him out of the Brig field as soon as maybe. It's too isolated. Just the sort of place where anything could happen to an animal and no one to say what caused it. The poor beast must submit to being mewed up in stables for a while until Master Wilfred's temper has had time to cool. Put him in the loose-box at the end near the coach house, and I'll move over to the groom's quarters above it. I'm a light sleeper. There'll be no attempt on him in the hours of darkness while I'm on guard."

Francesca looked more worried than ever. "You are very good," she said gratefully. "But how can I? The stables are not mine, despite Mr. Develyn's kindness. And how could I possibly explain the need for such a move? His own cousin!"

"And very little love lost between them, unless I miss my guess," returned Brandon shrewdly. "It's my belief that a mere hint would suffice for Mr. Develyn, and no doubt whose side he'd be on."

"Perhaps," conceded Francesca. "But to be provoking a quarrel between them is unthinkable."

There was a sharp frown for that. "There's a deal in what you say," Brandon acknowledged. "And his *lordship*"—there was bitter scorn in his pronouncement of the title—"a dead shot, and, in his present mood only too glad to salve his hurts with a little easy killing."

If Francesca had appeared anxious and alarmed before, this was a thought to banish every vestige of colour from a face that seemed frozen into a mask of fear. "Is he?" she managed at last, stiff lipped.

Brandon nodded. "A very fine shot indeed," he confirmed. And then, with a little smile, "I know of only two better—and both of them in this room. Mr. Develyn, by all accounts, was never more than workmanlike, though I've not seen him in action."

"But duelling is illegal," she protested desperately.

There was a suggestive silence. Then he said kindly, "Of course. You must forgive me, my dear. It was so much a commonplace in my younger days. I forget how much the times have changed—and in that respect, at least, for the better." And forebore to remind her that, legal or not, it was not so very long ago that so eminent a personage as the Duke of Wellington himself had engaged in a duel.

Between them they concocted a simple tale to explain the oddity of bringing in a horse from grass at this season. Francesca was to say that the nights were still chilly—there *had* been one or two cool ones—and that she feared that Merlin might take cold. Though what the stable staff would think of such a fantastic notion she said crossly, more confident now that she had a trusty ally in support, she did not care to think; for if ever an animal was in the pink of condition it was that same one who was to be brought indoors to be coddled in a warm stable. However, she acknowledged, they must tell some kind of a tale to explain to Mr. Develyn why the use of his loose-box was suddenly required. As for the accommodation over it, Brandon promised to have a word with Coates. The room was unused, so his occupation would bring no hardship to anyone but himself. He refused, with a twinkle, to tell her what tale he meant to spin to account for his peculiar whim, assuring her that what she did not know would not fret her. Francesca groaned. "Something cutting about unaccountable female fancies I suppose," she said resignedly. Brandon grinned, but refused to be drawn.

Since these ingenuous fables were designed chiefly for Mr. Develyn's delectation they might have spared themselves the pains. That gentleman had spent an uncomfortable and depressing afternoon following upon the departure of Wilfred, most formally and exquisitely attired, to call upon Francesca. A business call it might be, but it was plain that Wilfred meant to bring the full battery of his charm into play. And despite his own deepening dislike of the fellow, Robert knew very well that where the female sex was concerned that charm was formidable. If only he himself had not been so slow to know his own heart, or, having come at last to the truth, had been granted more time for his wooing without the distraction of Wilfred's presence.

As the afternoon wore on and his unwelcome guest did not return he found himself unable to settle to anything, and by the time that Jessop came to enquire if he should ask Cook to keep dinner back since his lordship was not yet come in, his concern had become acute. Fortunately, before he was called upon to pronounce a decision that would have infuriated the autocrat who ruled his kitchen and jeopardised his domestic comfort for a sennight, sounds of arrival were heard.

They were not the sounds normally associated with the arrival of a peer of the realm at a friendly house. The front door crashed open and slammed shut with a reverberating thump. There was the sound of sharp imprecation and the door opened and closed once more, his lordship, in his haste, having left the skirts of his driving coat in the door's close clasp. Jessop's eyes met his master's. "You may serve dinner as soon as his lordship comes down," said Robert. "No doubt he will wish to change his dress."

Jessop departed. Robert settled down to wait with what patience he might for what promised to be a singularly uncomfortable meal. Knowing Francesca and the high value she set upon Merlin he had not expected his cousin's errand to prosper. The manner of that cousin's return made him doubly thankful for his decision that Robin should have her supper in the schoolroom during Wilfred's visit instead of joining him at dinner as she did when they were alone. His small daughter was one female who had not capitulated to Wilfred's charm. Her father was bound to admit that there was some justification for his cousin's complaint that the child was too precocious by half and well on the way to becoming a proper little prig. But Wilfred's teasing was less than kind since it was invariably aimed at Robin's love of music. He knew perfectly well that the child disliked having anyone play her precious piano. Not all the extravagance of his lavish gifts could atone for the malice with which he deliberately abused the instrument under pretence of showing her how to produce various 'battle' effects. Robin would have to learn to accept teasing, and preferably before she went to school, but at times the misery in the small solemn face had brought Robert himself to the verge of protest. An odd quirk in a man's nature that made him take pleasure in tormenting anything so helpless and inoffensive. He glanced impatiently at the clock and wondered how soon the unwelcome guest would take his departure if his purpose in coming into Kent had failed of its achievement.

Dinner was disastrous. Because of the delay, one or two of the dishes were a little overcooked, though scarcely enough to signify since Mrs. Johnson, determined to do credit to her master in the judgement of his first house guest, invariably provided a choice of dishes that might have been judged adequate by Lucullus himself. Lord Finmore rejected the veal cutlets and the sweetbreads in cases with every appearance of loathing and picked languidly at a grilled pigeon. His expression was sullen, his response to every conversational gambit monosyllabic. Only his appreciation of the burgundy appeared undiminished. Jessop refilled his glass again and again but the wine seemed only to cast him into deeper gloom.

Despite his wish to show his cousin every observance proper from host to guest, Robert's patience was beginning to fray. Quietly he suggested that they should adjourn to the library and directed Jessop to bring in the brandy. When no other engagement intervened they had grown accustomed to lounging away the evenings there, sometimes in desultory conversation, more often beguiling the time with a rubber or two of piquet or a game of chess. Tonight his lordship made no pretence of the usual civilities. Contemptuously he refused every suggestion for his entertainment, tossed off a bumper of brandy with indecent haste, refilled his glass and began to prowl restlessly about the room. Robert watched him curiously, shoulders propped against the mantel shelf since it seemed discourteous to sit at ease until his guest was comfortably settled.

So this was the other face of the 'good fellow' who had made so famous an impression on local society. Behind the façade of genial charm was a peevish unlicked cub who sulked and fell into tantrums as soon as his will was crossed. Robert winced slightly as fingers grown clumsy with ill-temper handled a cherished vase of Samian ware which stood in a wall niche and replaced it with something perilously close to a crash. When, after making further inroads on the brandy, the same kind of abuse was extended to the library shelves, he could stand it no longer. Feeling much as Robin had felt at seeing her beloved piano so mishandled, he proceeded to draw the enemy's fire.

"You seem out of humor cousin. I take it that your suggestion of buying Merlin from Miss Thornish was ill-received."

"Miss Thornish!" Wilfred almost spat the name, in tones of virulent dislike. "Ill-conditioned upstart! Drab! Yes. She rejected my offer. She shall have cause to regret it!"

The threat implicit in the last part of this speech penetrated only vaguely into Robert's consciousness, since all his energies were absorbed in keeping a hold on his temper.

"You are speaking of a lady who has honoured me with her friendship," he said stiffly. "You will not refer to her in such terms in my hearing."

There was an ugly look on the Earl's handsome face. "Friendship?" he jeered. "D'you take me for a green 'un? Precious little of *friendship* between the pair of you, discreet as you've been while I've been here. I'll take leave to call the strumpet by whatever names I choose. *What* a honey-fall to inherit! House and lands and a well-taught mistress—even if the wench *is* a trifle long in the tooth for a discriminating palate. A lucky dog, ain't you, cousin?"

What more he might have chosen to add was lost in a crashing fall. Robert's hard-held control had snapped at last. Automatically, almost negligently, his left hand had bunched itself into a fist and struck hard and true on the sneering mouth that was pouring out its filthy abuse upon his darling.

The Earl lay where he had fallen, blood trickling from the corner of his mouth, a dazed expression on his face that was more the result of the brandy than of the blow, which had been no more than a smart jab.

"Get up," breathed Robert between tight lips. "It seems your education's been sadly neglected. Did they not teach you at Eton how to speak of a lady with proper respect? Let me endeavour to remedy the omission. Or if you are too dull to learn I can at least close your mouth for you so that it cannot betray you again."

The light of intelligence was back in the blue eyes. There was even a hint of a smile about the rapidly swelling lip.

"No thank you, cousin," returned the Earl politely. "I am perfectly comfortable in my present position. I was never your match when it came to fisticuffs. Even when I was warned of impending attack," he put in reflectively, and smiled again to see Robert flush at the justifiable criticism.

Heaven knew there had been provocation enough. Any man uttering such insults must surely expect retaliation. But it was true that his antagonist had been unprepared, perhaps off balance, when he had struck him down.

"If you feel that you have cause for complaint, I

am very willing to meet you when and where you chose," he said steadily.

The Earl clasped his hands behind his head and settled himself a little more comfortably. "You have been out of England over long, cousin," he explained kindly. "Duelling is quite out of favour in the best circles. A fortunate circumstance for *you*, I would point out. You may be my master with the small sword but I should naturally choose pistols and I should kill you without the least trouble—and, I may add, without the least regret. I never liked you, you know. But then I should be obliged to fly the country and that would not suit me at all. So—no meeting. You must assuage your wrath by ordering me out of your house. An order with which I will most willingly comply," he drawled, beginning to get to his feet. "For of all the insufferably boring habitations I have ever endured, commend me to a country house in Kent. And don't imagine that you have heard the last of *this*," he added with a sudden access of energy, laying a finger to his bruised mouth. "I am not in the habit of accepting such compliments without returning them in kind. When the time is ripe I will see that you are fully repaid."

Twelve

Robert could not help feeling that his cousin had really had the better of the encounter between them, and that in despite of that one satisfying 'facer'. But he was so thankful to be rid of him without an open and scandalous breach, so bent on pursuing the far more important business of courting Francesca, that he dismissed the ugly incident, threats and all, from his mind. As he made his way towards South Gates at the hour when they were accustomed to engage in a bout with the foils, he felt that the very air seemed lighter and fresher, lacking Wilfred's constricting presence.

With his foot on the doorstep, his hand outstretched to the bell-pull, he was brought up short. Somewhere quite close at hand two pistol shots rang out in swift succession. What, in heaven's name? Instinctively, after last night's interchange, he connected the sounds with Wilfred's talk of duelling. *Two* shots were strongly suggestive of a duel. But who—and where—and why?

The first essential was to ensure that Francesca was safe, and in no way concerned or alarmed by a sound so unusual in peaceful Saxondene. He pulled the bell with unusual vigour, puzzling the while as to the exact direction from which the sound of the shots had come. So close they had seemed, he almost believed that they had been fired within the boundaries of the park. But that *must* be nonsense.

He was so familiar a visitor by now that Marian admitted him without demur. But when he was shown into the quiet sunny room that he had come to know so well, only Mrs. Hornby was seated in one of the window embrasures where the light fell full on the delicate embroidery with which her hands were busy. She put up her work and smiled at him in greeting, proffered one or two amiable remarks as to the beauty of the morning, and explained that Francesca had just stepped out into the gardens for a little while with Brandon.

Robert looked perturbed. "Into the gardens?" he repeated. "I would not wish to alarm you ma'am, but as I came here just now I heard someone shooting. I hope——" Before he could finish the sentence two more shots rang out. And this time there could be no mistaking the fact that they had been fired just outside the window. Robert sprang up, but Mrs. Hornby only smiled comfortably and put a soothing hand on his arm.

"It *is* a shocking noise, isn't it?" she deprecated. "I'm sure I don't know how Francesca can do it, and never so much as blinks or jumps. But Brandon has been saying for an age that it was time she had the pistols out. His lordship—dear me—his *late* lordship

I *should* say—insisted that she practise regularly, you
know. Swords were all very well, he was used to say,
but how could a lady carry a sword wherever she
went? Or even a sword-stick? A pistol, now, is a very
different matter. He had a pair made specially for her,
so small and neat that she could slip one into the
pocket of a cloak or even into a muff or a reticule.
Brandon says they are beautiful weapons. But would
you not like to go out and see for yourself? He is very
proud of his pupil—though she is not so fine a shot
as he is, of course," she added, a lilt of quiet pride
in her voice that was pleasant to hear.

Robert, when he saw what Francesca could do with
her pretty little pistols, was inclined to think that
conjugal pride had swayed Mrs. Hornby's judgement.
Following her directions he had made his way to the
walk that led, in the lee of the park wall, to the South
Gates kitchen garden. Master and pupil were engaged
in earnest conversation when he arrived and it was
a moment or two before they saw him. He had time
to view and assess the unusual target they were using.
It was an accurate model of a large candelabrum
holding fourteen candles. Later he was to learn that
it had been devised by his uncle in mocking recollection of one of his youthful exploits when he had backed
himself to shoot out the flames of a number of genuine
candles. The figure that Uncle Miles had achieved was
not upon record. Rumour named it at anything between
a dozen and sixteen. But there was no doubt about
the abilities of his protégée and her tutor.

There had been a slightly startled air about them
when they saw Robert. Even, perhaps, a hint of guilt.
But that was easily understandable when Francesca

explained that, with the wind in this direction and the sound of the shots blanketed by the surrounding buildings, they had hoped he would not hear the noise they were making. They were eager to exhibit the beautiful workmanship of the pistols, to laugh over the oddity of the target and to tell him its story. All seemed fair and open, save that once they exchanged a glance that savoured of conspiracy; that Brandon, the dour recluse, was positively talkative; and that Francesca's manner betrayed a strain that could not be concealed from her lover's eyes by superficial gaiety.

Politely he admired the tiny weapons, examined the percussion mechanism which was unfamiliar to him and the trigger guard which locked the loaded pistol at the half cock position, but all the while his senses were alert to some queer undercurrent. When Francesca invited him to try his skill he laughed and shook his head. "What! Display my ineptitude before experts? No, I thank you! I was never more than mediocre. But do, pray, show me what you can achieve."

As simply as she had poured out her lovely voice for them when she was asked to sing, Francesca picked up one of the pistols which they had just reloaded. "Choose two numbers, then," she smiled at him. "Each candle is numbered, up to fourteen."

Robert chose numbers seven and thirteen and waited curiously, thinking that Brandon Hornby was standing a good deal closer to the target than was strictly prudent. Francesca's wrist came up smoothly and she fired twice. Brandon inspected the target critically.

"Clean through number seven but you only nicked thirteen," he called back to them.

They strolled up to the target to see for themselves, Francesca shaking her head over the poor second shot. "You're quite right, Brand," she said ruefully. "I really must try to find more time for practice."

"Gracious heavens, girl!" expostulated Robert. "If *I* could match your accuracy at this range, I should rather think it was my enemies who needed more practice!"

The oblique compliment quite failed of its intent. Francesca neither smiled nor disclaimed. She only furrowed her brow anxiously and said slowly, "Not if your enemy had the reputation of being a crack shot and quite ruthless to boot."

Robert's eyes narrowed in swift suspicion. He knew someone who answered very well to that description. But before he could enquire further, Brandon was asking if she meant to try again or if she felt she had done enough for one morning.

"Quite enough," she smiled at him. "I shall not so expose myself again until my eye is in. But do you, Brand, show how it should be done. A pity that the apples are not yet ready—we could have enacted the William Tell legend for you," she told Robert.

"Then I can only be thankful that they are not," he said bluntly. "*Your* nerves may be made of steel— mine could never endure such a spectacle. Indeed"— he grinned—"I thought Hornby was standing danger-ously close to the target when *you* were shooting."

She cried out indignantly at that and vowed that if he would but give her a week for practice she would back herself to 'put out' any of the target candles that he chose to name at a range of twenty five yards, but he only laughed and told her that he never staked his blunt against such odds. She seemed more relaxed and natural as together they watched Brandon dispose methodically of candle after candle. His detached precision was quite daunting. Robert found himself speculating curiously about the man's background and wondering what his history had been before the late Earl had introduced him into Francesca's service.

He expressed his appreciation of the performance in frank terms. "Miss Thornish need not fear the enemy she spoke of while she has you to protect her," he said pleasantly, "even if her own performance lacks something in accuracy, which to me, frankly, it did not. I have never in my life seen such shooting."

Brandon accepted the praise calmly, though modesty led him to point out that he was using familiar weapons of scrupulously exact design in an excellent light. Francesca said that she must go and wash the powder stains from her fingers but, rather surprisingly, did not invite Robert to accompany her back to the house. Hornby who had busied himself with taking down the target and putting the pistols back in their case said that he would clean and reload them for her and then covered her departure by asking if Robert could spare five minutes of his time to discuss another matter.

He then explained the measures that Francesca had taken for the well-being of the black colt. "I did not care to trouble you with the business last night, since it was already late when we brought him in, but if it is not convenient to have him occupying the loose-box, we can make some other arrangement," he concluded.

Robert eyed him thoughtfully. So Francesca feared for Merlin's safety, did she? He listened to the rather absurd tale that they had concocted without a blink and suggested solemnly that a groom had best sit up with the colt if he showed signs of developing a cough.

Brandon said, in some embarrassment, "Well, as to that, I'd thought of staying with him myself, if you've no objection to my moving over there for a night or two. I've a pretty fair notion of veterinary work and one doesn't want to take risks with a valuable animal like Merlin."

"No, indeed," agreed Robert gravely. "Nor with an unconscionable monomanic like my cousin Wilfred. And a pistol, in a steady hand, better medicine than draughts and boluses. You *do* take me for a slow-top, don't you? What does that poor child actually fear? Surely theft would not serve?"

Brandon heaved a sigh of relief. He was a man who liked everything open and above board. "More likely maiming," he said grimly. "If he can't own the beast himself he'll make sure no one else gets any good of him. And since Miss Francesca crossed his will he'll be wanting to make her suffer for it. I'm sorry to speak ill of your cousin but I know him better than you do and there's little I'd put past him."

Robert nodded thoughtfully. "Best keep the south gates locked during the hours of darkness," he suggested. "I'll see to the main gates. And keep Tara with you, if she won't make the colt nervous. She's a better guard than any sleepy groom—trained to it. As for my dear cousin—there's no love lost between us. In fact we had a bit of a turn-up last night and he's taken himself back to Town. You don't think he'll forget all about it when he cools off?"

Hornby shook his head. "Not he. And what's to be done in the long run is more than I can tell you, for

we can't keep the black mewed up for ever. A pity
Miss Francesca didn't agree to sell him, but she has a
particular fondness for the beast and she'll never consent to it now—not after the threats and the abuse
that his lordship indulged himself with."

They discussed the difficulties that they foresaw for
a few minutes more, but it was difficult to make firm
plans to meet so nebulous a threat. They settled it that
Francesca must not ride out alone, since both feared
that she might be in some personal danger or, at the
very least, exposed to unpleasant insult, and finally went
their separate ways in much increased esteem and good
will.

Several days passed with superficial tranquillity. The
weather was perfect and Francesca, at first inclined to
resent the idea of a curb on her freedom, thoroughly
enjoyed the actuality of her daily rides with Robert.
Merlin's training proceeded apace. He was at last
persuaded to accept Robert in the saddle. And a quaint
friendship had been struck up between the great black
stallion and his stable companion, Tara. Far from
being fretted by her presence, he now refused to settle
contentedly without her.

But though it was possible for a brief space to forget
one's anxieties in the exhilaration of a gallop over
the sweet smooth turf, return to Saxondene brought
back the sense of brooding uneasiness. Francesca did
her best to conceal the nervous fears that obsessed
her, But Robert had come to know her too well. The
swift turn of her head, the strain in her eyes at the
approach of any stranger, the suddenly stilled fingers,
the taut, listening attitude at any unusual sound, betrayed her all too plainly to the watchful eyes of love.

He did all that he could to support and comfort her, neglecting his work to be with her as much as possible, sharing the stable guard with Brandon so that both could snatch a few hours of sleep, and keeping vigilant watch over the comings and goings in the neighbourhood.

This, in itself, was no light task. The summer months were always the busiest on the roads for no one in his senses would travel in winter if it could be avoided. This was the season for paying family visits, and Robert sometimes thought that every dutiful son and daughter for miles around had suddenly decided to go and see that all was well with the old folks. To make matters worse, the approach of haysel had caused some of the larger farmers to take on extra labourers. This gave him considerable anxiety for many of these were rootless men, difficult to trace and identify. Wilfred was no fool. He would not send some city bred thug to implement his threats. He would choose a countryman, one who in speech and appearance would merge with his background and so could accomplish his fell intent and vanish again without attracting any particular notice. Any of these innocent-seeming labourers might well be Wilfred's man.

There were times, as one peaceful day succeeded another, when he would wonder if the danger lay only in their imaginings. It was hard to believe that a man of his own blood, one who had enjoyed every advantage of birth and breeding and education, could so demean his manhood as to insult and frighten a woman and plot to injure or kill a splendid young animal for no better cause than jealous spite. What if those words, uttered in the first shock of disappointment, were quite forgotten by now?

Hardest of all to endure was the inevitable delay in his wooing of Francesca. With every passing day he loved her more tenderly. He loved her the more that she was no longer the glowing girl whom he had escorted to the masquerade. She was sleeping badly and the marks of it showed in the shadows beneath her eyes and the listless droop of her shoulders when she thought herself unobserved. He longed to pour out his love upon her, to win her back to smiles and confidence, secure in the haven of his keeping, and he dared not attempt it. As things stood she trusted him unreservedly, turning to him with a naturalness that rejoiced his heart. But that did not mean that she was ready for love and marriage or that she regarded him as anything more than a dependable ally. Until her present anxieties were resolved he could not put forward a plea that might only distress her and cause her to withdraw a little when most she needed him. So he was at considerable pains to preserve the attitude of frank comradeship to which he felt she trusted, never dreaming how often she longed for the comfort of strong arms holding her close.

At the end of a week he was able to dismiss one, at least, of the doubts that had troubled him. They were given an unpleasant reminder that Wilfred had neither forgotten nor repented his rash threats.

Robin was in the habit of wandering down through the park to meet Miss Marsden on her way from the Rectory. On this particular morning she came running back alone to say that Miss Thornish would like to consult Papa on a matter of some urgency. Miss Marsden appearing at this point the two of them went into the house to begin the morning's lessons while Robert strode off swiftly in the direction of South Gates.

But as he passed the charming little folly that had been made out of the original south lodge he caught the sound of a choking sob. Turning aside he climbed the steps that led to the open doorway of the summer house and glanced inside. The scene that met his eyes needed no explanation. Francesca was sitting on one of the marble benches with which the place was furnished, her head down on the arm which rested on the table in front of her, her other hand so tightly clenched that the knuckles showed white as she strove to force back the sobs which were shaking her slender shoulders. On the floor at her side lay the stiffened body of the vixen, Reyna, the mask hideously wrinkled in the death agony.

Robert forgot everything but the woeful, tear-stained face that she raised at the sound of his footsteps. He crossed the little pavilion in two swift strides, picked her up bodily and sat down with her in his arms, cradling her like a child, her face buried in his shoulder. He held her so, quietly, until the storm of sobs gradually subsided. Then he said gently, "Come now, my little love. You have grieved enough. It is time to dry your tears and put on a brave face again."

Since the only answer she vouchsafed was to burrow her face more deeply into his breast, he resorted to stronger measures, holding her a little away from him and tilting up her chin with kindly fingers, pulling out his own handkerchief and drying her cheeks as he might have done Robin's.

"It is bad for you to cry so much," he told her gravely. And then, seeing her a little calmer, went on,

"Besides, you are making my coat shockingly wet. I daresay I shall take a dreadful cold!"

That evoked a very watery chuckle that was still perilously close to a sob, but it seemed that Francesca was on the road to recovery. With no regard whatever for the impropriety of such behaviour in one who was neither a close relative nor an affianced husband, Robert settled her more comfortably into his hold, stroked back one or two strands of hair that clung to her brow, stooped to kiss the brow itself and the tear swollen eyelids with firm comforting lips and said, "Now tell me all about it."

When you are a little taller than the average woman, have prided yourself for years on your independent disposition and your ability to get along very well without men, it is a novel experience to be addressed as "little love" and picked up as easily as though you were still a slip of a girl. When, in addition, you have been a stranger to demonstrations of affection since nursery days, it is utterly disarming to be 'babied'— that was how Francesca described it to herself—as though you were a forlorn child. But strange as these sensations were, she very much enjoyed them. In that blissful moment she felt herself infinitely fragile and feminine and precious. She snuggled herself contentedly into Robert's hold, even ventured to put up one shy hand to touch the lapel of his coat, and embarked upon her story.

At this season of the year she was in the habit of spending the forepart of the morning in the summer house. It caught the early morning sun and gave a delightful prospect across the Italian garden to the trees of the park. This morning she had carried writing materials with her, meaning to write to Armi. The stiffened body of the dead vixen had been propped up so that at first, in the dimmer light of the pavilion, she had not realised that the creature was dead. She had even spoken to her by name. Then, in putting down her writing case, she had moved the table slightly and the vixen's body had toppled over on its side. At the same moment she had seen Robin skipping gaily down the avenue and in sending the child off on her errand had thought to spare her a shocking and distressful sight.

Robert laid his cheek lovingly against her hair. "Poor wretched animal," he said pitifully. "But thanks to you she had her life and her freedom for a little while. And she has served you well in dying since now we are left in no doubt about the threat to Merlin. So let us take order about the next move. No more of this independent nonsense, my darling! I'll have you safe at Saxondene right away. And Mrs. Hornby, too, of course." But it was regrettably plain that this was the merest after-thought, and whether he required Mrs. Hornby's attendance for that lady's own comfort or solely to appease propriety was a point that remained in doubt.

It was positively painful to break out of the comforting cocoon in which she felt herself enwrapped, but Francesca made the necessary effort.

"You—you believe this to be Lord Finmore's work?" she said hesitantly.

"Through the agency of some hired minion—yes. He must have heard the tale of Reyna a dozen times at least during his sojourn here. It was too good a joke to be missed. He would guess your fondness for her— and this is his way of striking at *you*. That she might

be poisoned or shot by any farmer who took exception
to her depredations, I'd allowed for. Only hoped you'd
never discover her true fate," he added, a trifle shamefaced. "But if that had been the case she would not
have been brought here to confront and shock you.
The killer would have buried the body or thrown it
on some midden. No. This is Wilfred's hand. And he's
a bigger fool than I had thought, giving us warning
of his intent. For the job was done by someone who
knows the ways of the place. Yes! And by someone
who was able to enter here despite locked gates."

"And the intent is to kill Merlin—as he killed
Reyna?" she queried bravely, her voice still raw with
tears.

He nodded reluctantly. "Kill—or maim," he answered. "Probably the latter, since it would leave to
you the agonising necessity of having the poor brute
destroyed. It's no use wearing blinkers. But now that
we are forewarned they'll not find it so easy." His brow
creased in thought, though there was a hint of a rueful
smile about his mouth. He could not help reflecting
that it was a sad pity there was no time to teach the
girl in his arms a little more of what she meant to
him, a little more about the ways of love. He could
think of few pleasanter ways of spending a fine summer's morning. But other matters must take precedence.
Until the menace that threatened their peace had been
thoroughly scotched, he had best devote his energies
to dealing with dear Cousin Wilfred.

Taking Brandon Hornby into their conclave they
eventually evolved a plan that seemed likely to block
the success of any attack on the black colt. More than
that they could not do, since no one could say when

the attempt might come or what form it would take.
Having agreed that the hours of darkness were likely
to prove the most dangerous, it was decided that the
two men should keep double watch over the stable
from darkening till dawn. Robert and Francesca between them would be responsible for the colt's exercise
while Brandon snatched a few hours' sleep, and Robert
would take what rest he could in the afternoons. Brandon agreed that he would be easier in his mind knowing
that his wife would be safely tucked away in the big
house with Francesca. Not that he anticipated any
personal attack on either of them, but down at South
Gates they would feel cut off from events and would
suffer miseries of anxiety in just waiting for news.

A careful examination of the park boundary eventually showed how last night's intruder had made his
entry. An overhanging beech bough had given him a
hand-hold to pull himself up to the top of the wall. A
patch of moss had been ripped away from the wall by
feet seeking a firm purchase and two deep imprints in
the soft mould showed where he had dropped down
from the wall top. A tuft of reddish hairs still adhering
to the brickwork of the wall probably indicated the
place where the vixen's body had been dragged after
him.

"Must have used a rope," grunted Robert, studying
the evidence. "Now, do we take that bough off right
away—it needs trimming back in any case—or do we
leave our friend to think himself secure in using the
same means of access again?"

"If I had *my* way, I'd leave it just as it is and set a
man-trap *there*," said Brandon sourly, nodding at the
spot where the intruder had landed.

Francesca exclaimed in horror. Robert said swiftly, "No. Not a man-trap. As likely to catch the innocent as the guilty."

She sighed her relief. "You *could* not approve anything so treacherous and cruel," she agreed, and cast a reproachful glance at Brandon.

"Don't go setting me on too high a form, my girl," Robert warned her. "I may not care for the notion of using a man-trap, but don't imagine I'll show any mercy if I get my hands on the brute who caused you such distress. Or better still on my precious Cousin Wilfred. It would afford me infinite satisfaction to deal with such gentry as they deserve."

These bloodthirsty sentiments met with a degree of approval surprising in a gently bred female who was squeamish about man-traps. Though little or nothing had been said, the discovery that her love for Robert was returned with interest had done much to restore Francesca to her normal spirits. She was still deeply concerned for Merlin's well-being, but she saw the difficulties, now, through a haze of happiness. As they turned to go back to the house she slipped a hand confidingly into Robert's. "*That* you may do with my very good will," she told him, smiling up into his face with such a glow of adoration in her eyes that Brandon Hornby, suddenly enlightened, had some ado to refrain from proffering his felicitations on the spot.

Thirteen

That first joyous rapture dimmed a little. Three days passed. No further word of love was spoken. Robert's every action witnessed to his care for his lady, but Francesca, inexperienced in the ways of love and still a little dazed and incredulous, would have liked the reassurance of words. And then she saw so little of him. Only at morning exercise, when his attention was largely preoccupied by his responsibility as escort, and, briefly, in the evenings if she chose to visit the stables. And there they were never alone. Their talk centred mainly on such topics as the incidence of strangers in the vicinity and how long it might be necessary to remain in a state of virtual siege. There was no place for the happy planning of a shared future in which Francesca longed to indulge. And Armi was due to arrive in four days' time which must even further restrict the commerce between them. It was going to be a delicate business explaining to Armi why she had suddenly removed from South Gates to the big house. The threat to Merlin, alone, was scarcely adequate reason, and since Robert had said nothing of marriage plans it seemed likely that Armi would pose a number of interested enquiries that Francesca would be unable to answer.

Between the two men who shared the stable guard, liking deepened into firm friendship. Despite the difference in age there was a growing affinity between them. The hours that they kept watch were long ones and they sat in darkness, hoping by this means to lull the enemy into a sense of false security. Every half hour or so by the chime of the stable clock one or other would slip out quietly to patrol the approaches to the buildings, with particular attention directed towards the park wall where a certain beech tree still extended a friendly arm to offer assistance to night visitors. In the intervals between these patrols they relied mainly on Tara to give them early warning of any alien approach. But it was essential to keep awake and alert. The hours they could snatch for sleep were insufficient and the stable atmosphere, sweet with the scent of hay and disturbed only by the peaceful movements of well kept and contented beasts was distinctly soporific. So to keep themselves awake, they talked. And such talk, their voices muted, their faces invisible, approached intimacy with confident strides that would have been unimaginable in normal conditions. They were brothers-in-arms, enlisted in the same cause. Man spoke to man in the quiet stable—and liked very well what he found.

Their talk ranged over the whole field of human endeavour. Perhaps, at first, Robert took the lead. It was easy to talk on such impersonal matters as his various journeys and explorations. And he soon discovered in Brandon Hornby a percipient and critical mind, well able to evaluate the importance of such finds as were not, in the vulgar sense, treasure.

Presently Brandon grew more expansive about his own travels and they compared notes about places and peoples that both knew. The Earl of Finmore's name—the late Earl's—began to creep into the conversation with growing frequency. They applauded his social address and chuckled over some of his more acid comments until almost it seemed that he was there with them, a third member of their invisible brotherhood. So relaxed and easy did they become in each other's company that the bounds of normal reticence were sometimes overstepped. Perhaps it was not really surprising that, after chuckling over a drily humorous account of one of his uncle's adventures, Robert should find himself saying idly, "How did you first come to meet Uncle Miles?"

Even as the words passed his lips he wished them unsaid. It was no business of his. And though the question was innocent enough he had sensed in Brandon a deep devotion to the dead man that argued no ordinary friendship. Instinct had warned him not to pry too closely lest he waken old sorrows to distress one whom he had judged as decent a fellow as ever stepped. Now a careless slip of the tongue had sent him blundering in. He heard the sharp-caught breath, felt the weight of the momentary pause as though it pressed upon his own spirit.

The stable clock chimed the half hour. He got up thankfully. "Time to go the rounds again," he began.

"Yes," said Brandon quietly. And then, laconically, "I first met your uncle on the Holyhead road. I held him up."

It was Robert's turn to be shocked into momentary silence. Then, irresistibly, a low chuckle of deep amusement escaped him. He should have expected the unexpected. Such an encounter—and such an outcome —was perfectly characteristic, both of Uncle Miles and of the man he was coming to know so well.

In the darkness there was a note of content in Brandon's voice. "You are very like him, you know. Oh—you will never be the man that he was. We moderns are too docile, too law-abiding to achieve that sort of stature. He was—he was 'grand seigneur'." He paused a moment as though that summed up everything. "But when you laughed just now, you might have been his lordship's self. And your ways are very much his ways. I know, now, why he chose you to inherit Saxondene. *And* the care of Miss Francesca." Another pause. Then, more briskly, "But—as you said —time to look around. If all is quiet, then the tale of that first meeting may serve to beguile an hour of this interminable waiting."

The moon, three quarters full, was just rising. Had Robert been planning a marauding raid in hostile territory he would have chosen just such a night. Sufficient light to pick one's way accurately, the shadows dense enough to afford good cover. But nothing moved. Only the hunting cry of a barn owl broke the stillness of the night. He made his rounds undisturbed and came softly back again. Brandon took up his story.

"I will not bore you with all the mistakes and misfortunes that drove me to so desperate a course," he said drily. "A man is always swift to excuse his own failings and the tale of them makes dull hearing. Briefly, then, I was educated with a view to entering the Church. The uncle for whom I am named had a living in his gift, and since the present incumbent was well advanced in years it was understood that in due time I would succeed him. To be honest, I had no real calling to the priesthood. The arrangement was one of those family affairs and since I was a younger son with no prospects and no particular talent, I was well enough pleased to fall in with it. Meanwhile I secured congenial employment as private chaplain to a certain nobleman who shall remain nameless. I was also tutor to his sons, librarian and, at times, secretary. A busy life, but a pleasant one. Still my appointment to the family living was delayed. When the time came for my eldest pupil to make the Grand Tour his father did me the honour of inviting me to accompany him. He was naturally cognisant of my circumstances and, rather than appoint a new tutor had decided to send the two younger boys to school. The temptation was irresistible. I had a certain aptitude for languages but I had never travelled abroad and I embarked on the venture with the happiest of anticipations and never a backward glance. My mother had died while I was still at school, my father was perfectly indifferent to my proceedings, caring only for his gaming and his racing. And for five months my pupil and I took both pleasure and profit from our travels."

He broke off and sat silent awhile, as though looking back at the past and rearranging his thoughts. Then he said slowly, "You will forgive me that I prefer not to name names after so many years. Old wrongs should be allowed to remain buried. Your uncle had the whole truth out of me at our first meeting and I think his acceptance of my veracity will accredit me with you. It was in Vienna that I met Catherine."

Again he paused for a moment or two, then went on steadily, "She was a girl of gentle birth who had been governess in a family ranking high in diplomatic circles. But she had been dismissed from her post and, when first we met, had been brought so low as to attempt the crime of self-destruction. What else, she asked me, when my frantic efforts had restored her to consciousness, was left to one who had neither friends nor money nor reputation? And reproached me bitterly for not allowing her to drown."

The silence was longer this time. They heard the 'hoo-hoo' of the owl as it drifted overhead. Brandon said briskly, "My turn to take a look outside." For a moment his shadow was flung behind him across the pool of white moonlight that marked the mouth of the archway. Then he was gone into the darkness beyond. Knowing in advance the end of the story, Robert still could not imagine how it had been brought about. Nor could he associate thoughts of desperate drama with placid comfortable Mrs. Hornby, who so dearly loved a good game of whist. But he would have staked his own hopes of happiness on the integrity of the man who was telling the tale.

He was still pondering the emotional experiences that might lie behind the most homely, the most smooth-seeming surfaces when Hornby came quietly back.

"All's quiet," he reported briefly, and addressed himself again to his story. "I could not abandon the child—she was little more—lest somehow she contrive to achieve her dreadful purpose. I will not weary you with all the shifts I was put to, to find a respectable lodging for my soaking half-drowned waif. Suffice it that there is still kindliness and Christian charity in the world. The baker's wife who took her in and nursed her so tenderly for the modest sum that was all I could afford will surely win her reward. But twice more during the weeks that followed Catherine tried to put an end to herself. I watched her as best I could, torn between my duty to my charge and a growing tenderness for the desolate girl whose sole dependence was on me. The time was fast approaching when I must leave Vienna. Our arrangements were made to return by leisurely stages to Salzburg and then into Switzerland before re-visiting Paris and returning to England. It was manifestly impossible to add my protégée to the party, yet I could not bring myself to desert her. A fortunate chance, as I thought at the time, offered me a possible solution. A young neighbour, a friend of my pupil's arrived in Vienna in charge of *his* tutor, a gentleman with whom I was slightly acquainted. Though I did not know him intimately he was perfectly reliable and respectable and after careful consideration I persuaded him to take over my responsibilities to my pupil. Everyone seemed quite content with the arrangement and I was able to devote myself to my poor Catherine, promising that as soon as I had carried her safely home to England I would make all speed to inform my employer of the reasons for my strange conduct and of the arrangements that I had made for his son. He had always been both generous and reasonable and I had good hopes of winning his forgiveness for my desertion of my post."

Tara came to the door of the loose-box and whined to be let out. The two men listened intently but could hear nothing untoward. Softly Robert lifted the latch and the boarhound disappeared into the night but at a leisurely pace that suggested preoccupation with private affairs rather than a threat of attack.

They listened, but all was silent. After a few moments Tara came back and settled down beside her master with a grunt and a sigh of content.

"Supper?" suggested Robert.

They ate the juicy beef sandwiches with which they had fortified themselves against the night's watch. Robert bit into an apple, but it was wizened and tasteless. He rejected it, saying that he would be thankful when the new crop was ready.

"Was a time when Cathy and I would have been thankful enough for withered apples, honestly come by," retorted Brandon, chewing on his own apple. "Things went smoothly enough at first though the journey took much longer than I had anticipated. Since the days that I speak of I've travelled far and wide with his lordship, but there's a vast difference between travelling under the aegis of wealth and consequence and making one's own humble way without that support. Catherine was unwell—she is always poor traveller. And I had not the means to alleviate her discomfort, even though I had felt myself obliged to accept a generous parting gift from my erstwhile pupil. Of necessity we travelled slowly. Too slowly. By the time we reached home the news of our coming had run ahead of us."

"And changed beyond recognition in doing so?" suggested Robert sympathetically.

"It had retained just sufficient of the truth to make it impossible of denial," agreed Brandon grimly. "Some mischief-maker in Vienna had made it his business to inform my patron that I had neglected my duties for weeks before deserting my post to run off with a young woman of ill repute." For the first time the quiet voice betrayed emotion. The last words gritted out. "We never discovered who the tale-bearer was, though I had my suspicions. There was one that bore a grudge against me because I'd helped Catherine to slip through his fingers. Always hoped I'd get to grips with him one day but the luck didn't favour me. By the time I was in a position to track him down he was dead—killed in a drunken brawl they told me. But the damage was done. My employer pointed out that I had dismissed myself from his service and that under the circumstances he owed me nothing and certainly could not give me a reference. He had carried the tale to my family. My father cared little enough about my morals but since he had been having some over-deep doings at the tables was glad of so plain an excuse to cast me off with every sign of righteous indignation. My brother who had taken over the management of our Lincolnshire estate was willing to house me but would not permit his wife to receive Catherine. No doubt he had his hands full wringing a bare living out of that unthankful soil after years of my father's mismanagement. My Uncle Brandon washed his hands of me, pointing out that I was obviously unfitted to have the care of a parish. I heard later that he now intended the living for his own second son who, poor devil, had been forced to abandon a promising military career after losing a leg.

"Fortunately I had friends of the humbler sort who were less nice in their notions—some who were even prepared to believe my story. But one cannot sponge on one's friends indefinitely. I stayed in Lincolnshire only long enough to arrange my marriage to Catherine. She was an orphan with no one to turn to. Though when you consider the treatment I received from *my* family, perhaps it is not so vast a deprivation!"

Robert's thoughts turned for a moment to another young girl who had received but scurvy treatment from those who should have sheltered and protected her. But Francesca had at least been financially secure. Poor little Catherine!

"As soon as our marriage was accomplished I took my wife to London and started to look for work. You can imagine the rest. Without a reference and increasingly threadbare as I sold everything that was not absolutely essential in order to buy food, I soon found that all the professions were closed to me, even in their lowest ranks. My only other talent was a certain facility with small sword and pistols, and thanks to this I at last found employment in a school of arms. There was a good deal of menial work involved as well as the instruction but I did not mind that. At least I had got a start in a new life. Our landlady—a kindly soul if rough-tongued—found some sewing work for Cathy through a friend in the dressmaking line and we ventured to hope that the worst of our troubles were over. Alas! My school was a small and undistinguished one, the pupils drawn mainly from what I can only describe as the 'mushroom' class. Perhaps I tried too hard— so anxious as I was to make a good impression. I put all I knew into giving them the best possible advice, but my manners did not find favour. Not that I was ever rude or insolent. But at the end of a month my master informed me that I was paid to encourage the pupils, not to depress their pretensions, and I was dismissed. I touched bottom then. I actually pleaded with the fellow to keep me on, promising to mend my ways, but he refused. His best paying client had complained of my 'superior' way of correcting his sword play. It was a choice between us."

"Was that when you took to the road?" demanded Robert, so carried away by his interest in the story that he forgot to lower his voice.

Brandon hushed him sharply. Then laughed softly in the darkness. "You see? That was what they complained of! I gave orders—instead of politely suggesting."

"Tell me how you held up Uncle Miles."

Brandon chuckled softly. "What a complete hand he was! If I had known him—if I had even known who was driving that phaeton, for of course I knew of him, by repute. But I was completely green. And one man driving a phaeton—not even a groom—seemed easy meat, even if he *was* driving a bang-up team. I took him for some young Corinthian—regular out-and-outer —and cursed my luck, not expecting him to be particularly plump in the pocket. I pulled him up about a mile beyond Hadley Highstone—nothing in sight either way—and bade him hand over his purse.

" 'Very willing to oblige you, my good fellow,' he said, in that lazy voice of his. I came to know it well— and to know that he was ever most dangerous when he sounded most vague and sleepy. 'But I don't carry one. Spoils the set of one's coat, y'know. If you care for such things. But perhaps you don't?' He seemed prepared to discuss the matter at length but I was nervous as a cat and anxious to be done with him and away. I growled out something about not expecting me to believe that he travelled without a guinea in his pockets and to hand over the dibs in short order.

" 'Well—yes, and no,' he drawled at me. 'Not in my pockets, you see. I keep 'em in the strong-box, here, beside me.' And he nudged it with his foot. 'Would it be troubling you too much to help yourself? This team of mine won't stand.' And I could see for myself they were dancing and fretting and would like as not make a bolt for it if he didn't keep them in hand. Yes— you may laugh! How was I to know he was a regular top-sawyer?

" 'It's not locked,' he told me encouragingly, 'and best make haste or that chaise will be up with us, and I imagine you don't want that!'

"I told you I was green as grass, didn't I? All his finicky talk had bewildered me, strung up and scared as I was. There *was* no chaise, of course. But just for a second I glanced up, in the direction he had indicated. It was enough! The next thing I knew I was coming to myself, propped up in a chair in my lord's library in London house. And this time it was my lord who held my pistol.

" 'New to the game?' he enquired gently when he saw that I had recovered my wits.

"I didn't answer. I didn't even wonder why he hadn't simply handed me over to the nearest constable.

All my thoughts were for Cathy. What would become of her when I was brought to book for my crimes? The child would be born soon. I could only pray that our landlady would take pity on her.

" 'And do you habitually conduct your—er—enterprises with unloaded weapons?' enquired his lordship pleasantly.

"I mumbled something about not wishing to kill him, he having done me no harm. He laughed at that. 'You esteem your marksmanship pretty high, my friend. If you succeeded in killing me with *this* antiquated piece, it would be, I think, by accident!'

"Somehow that flicked me on the raw. A man has his quirks of pride, even when he is sunk as low as I was. There was a branch of candles standing at his elbow. I told him I would undertake to extinguish their flames with that very pistol that he so maligned. It had belonged to my grandfather and was, indeed, well-worn, but I knew its every trick.

" 'This we must see,' decided his lordship, much amused. 'It so chances that I have some reputation in that line myself. But 'tis a matter will keep. To speak truth, I do not care for the notion of putting a loaded pistol into your hands at this range. You might, you see, miss the candles. I would prefer to know a little more about you first. Tell me—when did you last eat?'

"If I had answered him, it had been at breakfast on the previous day, and little enough at that. But I was beyond speech. The brief flare of annoyance over my marksmanship had finished me. The candles grew misty in my sight, his lordship's face a monstrous wavering mask, and I disgraced myself utterly by fainting dead away like some greensick girl."

There was such disgust in his tone as he related this part of the story that Robert could not help smiling. But he was careful to allow no trace of amusement to appear in his voice as he prompted gently, "And then?"

"He tended me—himself—as though I had been his own son," said Brandon brusquely. He still could not bear to linger over this part of the story. "Oh—he had the whole tale out of me—cursed me roundly for every kind of a fool—threatened to give me the thrashing I deserved for my impudence in thinking I could hold *him* up—and offered me a job as his personal courier. Even convinced me that he really needed one," and Robert could hear the wry grin in the quiet voice.

There was a long silence. Then Brandon said abruptly, "Catherine's baby—a girl—was a frail little thing. She lived only a few weeks. Perhaps the sufferings that her mother had undergone had sapped her strength. When, years later, his lordship came to enlist our sympathies for his latest waif, you can imagine how gladly we consented. And the girl herself won our hearts. She has taken the place of the children we never had."

Robert had wondered about that, guessing that the frail infant whom Brandon described so impersonally was not *his* child. What tragedy lay behind Catherine Hornby's placid face he would never know—but little wonder that she had attempted suicide. Yet there could be no mistaking the steadfast love and trust between the pair. They had found true happiness after their sufferings. As he and Francesca would do, he thought contentedly, once this wretched business with Cousin Wilfred was settled.

And even on the thought heard the warning rumble in Tara's throat and felt the hackles rise beneath his silencing hand.

Fourteen

The plan of the defenders was a simple one. They had two primary objects in mind. Brandon, infinitely the better shot, was charged with the task of guarding the black colt, though he would shoot only in the last resort and then to disable rather than to kill. To Robert, younger and more active, was assigned the interception and capture of the intruder. Somehow they must endeavour to establish Lord Finmore's responsibility for these outrages, and the best hope of obtaining the evidence they sought was to lay hands upon his agent. Without such evidence, evidence so clear and indisputable that a threat to publish it would bind the Earl to submission, the present menace to Merlin's safety and Francesca's peace of mind might persist indefinitely.

It was for this reason that the main door at the end of the archway that gave access to the stable yard had been left so invitingly open—the door itself fastened back as it always was during the daytime in the heat of summer, to suggest that some careless groom had simply forgotten to close it at dusk. That wide-propped door offered an obvious avenue of escape for a hard-pressed fugitive and Robert was stationed there to prevent just such an escape. Beyond this they could make no exact dispositions. There was no saying how the attack might develop. Each must use his own judgement over coming to the aid of the other in case of need.

If tonight's visitor was aware of that conveniently open door, he evidently suspected a trap and declined its innocent invitation, for the small noises that indicated his stealthy approach came, not from the direction of the archway but from almost directly over their heads.

"Must have squeezed through the window in the groom's quarters," said Brandon in Robert's ear, his voice no more than a breath. "Means to come down through the trap door into the loose-box itself. Very well informed, our visitor." He vanished from Robert's side as silently as he had appeared. The furtive sounds overhead continued. Above the pounding of the blood in his ears Robert heard the soft click as Brandon cocked his pistol and then another, different click which puzzled him for a moment until he realised that his friend had shuttered the dark lantern.

They had reckoned that any marauder confronted by an alert guardian, pistol in hand, would probably take to his heels without trying to press home his attack. This would give Robert his opportunity. And at first it seemed as if the plan would work out just as they had hoped. From his concealment Robert could hear the uneasy movements of the colt, well aware that something strange was afoot and restless and curious as a consequence. There was a shrill, grating noise as the bolts that secured the trap door, long unused, were dragged back. A moment later came a confusion of sounds from within the loose-box and at the same instant a soft glow of light illumined the half-door.

Poised for action, Robert heard Brandon's crisp, "Stay where you are or I shoot." What more he might have said was drowned in the wild squeal of the young stallion, startled to fury by the sudden descent of a stranger almost under his nose. In the lantern's dim light Robert saw him rear up, crest tossing, teeth bared, forefeet trampling the air. Then a dark-clad figure flung himself over the half-door, dropped to the ground and plunged for the archway.

The door of the loose-box opened as Brandon followed, letting out a stream of light that silhouetted the fugitive. Robert, tensed to spring, saw the dull gleam of steel in the man's hand and swerved to his left, going for the knife hand instead of taking the fellow round the knees as he had thought to do. It was unfortunate that Tara, delighted by so clear an invitation to action, should, at the same moment, have launched herself at the intruder's throat. Collision between master and hound was inevitable. Each was thrown a little off balance and neither attained the intended target. All three protagonists crashed to the ground, their impetus carrying them clear of the archway and out into the stable yard. Tara, foiled of her intended throat-hold, sank her teeth in a shoulder, but thanks to a modishly padded coat got little good of it. Robert found himself clutching his opponent round the waist. The only advantage he had gained was in bringing his man to grass, and since his own left arm was pinned under the fellow's body, it was a slight one.

He managed to wrench himself free as his antagonist heaved away from him, the hand that held the knife striking at Tara. Robert's right arm, flung across his body, prevented the first attempt from being fully effective. It struck the hound a glancing blow on the neck but she did not release her hold. As it was drawn back to strike again, two things happened simultaneously. A shot rang out. There was a metallic clang as the knife spun out of fingers numbed by the impact. And Robert, half sitting, half lying, brought over his right fist to the point of his enemy's jaw with sufficient force to put him *hors de combat* for some time.

Tara released her hold at the word of command and came to sit meekly at her master's feet that he might examine her hurts. Only when he had satisfied himself that the knife slash, though bleeding freely, was no more than skin deep did he glance up at Brandon and say, "Very pretty shooting, friend. My thanks for it, and Tara's. And my most fervent gratitude to the providence that chanced to enlist us on the same side. If ever I'm fool enough to quarrel with you, remind me to insist on swords!"

"Which would be weighted even more unequally in *your* favour, and a protracted agony at that," retorted Brandon. "At least shooting is a quick death. But never mind exchanging compliments. Let's have this fellow under cover before he comes round. It's just possible that someone may have heard the shot and will come to investigate, and I, for one, would prefer to dispense with an audience for our inquisition."

There was a grim note in his voice that boded ill for the captive if he should prove obdurate. Between them they carried him into the stable and dumped him ungently in an empty stall. Brandon brought the lantern and a halter rope and they secured his arms to his body but still he showed no signs of returning consciousness.

"Might as well go through his pockets before he wakes up," grunted Brandon. And then, with a reminiscent grin, "I'll see to that, being something of a professional."

Robert laughed. "I'll expect to hear all about your exploits in that line," he warned, "once we're through with this business," and began to kindle a second lantern from the wick of Brandon's.

"That will not take over-long," Brandon told him, methodically removing the contents of the prisoner's pockets. "His lordship was only my second—er—client. The first was a farmer riding home from market. From him I took his sorry nag since a horse was essential to my new career. The fellow thought me mad because I did not demand his purse as well. I often wondered what became of that poor beast, and hoped he had made his way home after his lordship turned him loose."

The lantern was glowing steadily. "I'll go and find that knife," Robert said. "Then I'll help you look through those."

The knife had slid across the paved yard, carried by the force with which it had been struck from the intruder's hand, and come to rest against a drinking trough. It took Robert a minute or two to find it. He examined it curiously. It was no ordinary weapon. He judged it to be very old. But despite its decorative hilt and beautifully damascened blade it was still capable of dealing death. The steel, its silver inlay spoiled now by the furrow which Brandon's bullet had made, was razor sharp. It struck Robert as curious that a man should choose so distinctive a weapon for so secret a purpose. He carried it back to the stable, turning it thoughtfully between his hands.

Inside the stable Brandon had finished his task. The prisoner was showing signs of returning consciousness. Brandon glanced up as Robert added the dagger to the collection of oddments that his ally had set out neatly on the window ledge.

"Next time we'll remember to search a man *before* we tie him up," he said laconically. "I'd the devil's own job getting at the inside pockets. And nothing that's of use to us to show for it, unless there's anything in his papers." He nodded at a slightly shabby pocket book that he had put to one side. "Now, let's have this mask off him and see what we've caught."

He ripped off the mask that covered the prisoner's face, heedless of a protesting groan as he pulled it down over a rapidly swelling jaw, stared for a moment as though unable to believe his eyes, and then said amazedly, "O'Malley! Great God in Heaven! You, of all men, to come to horse maiming!"

The sound of his own name seemed to recall the prisoner's wandering wits. He opened his eyes and tried to sit up, but was prevented by his bonds. Robert stiffened. "*Hugh* O'Malley?" he asked sharply.

Brandon nodded. "That same. You've heard of him, I see. A versatile rascal with no morals, fewer scruples and but the one redeeming grace—or so I'd have said until tonight—his love of horses. To find him here upon such an errand is the last thing I'd have believed."

"And it's in the right of it you'd have been," put in O'Malley coolly. "If ye're thinking I meant harm to the colt, ye're sadly mistaken."

Robert stared down at him. Despite bonds and bruises he looked quite untroubled, even cheerful. And this was the villain who had drugged and abducted Francesca, and she little more than a child. There was a slow rage burning within him, a rage that must be held in check, since one could not maltreat a helpless prisoner.

"You must forgive us," he said with biting courtesy. "Circumstantial evidence, alas! One should *never* rely upon it—or so I have frequently been told. I am sure that you can give a perfectly reasonable explanation for your presence here tonight. I can only offer my sincere regrets that your welcome was not all that it might have been. Had I but known in good time who my cousin would choose as his envoy, I would have done my poor best to meet the occasion."

O'Malley had rolled over to stare at him, his mouth agape. "The divil's in it!" he exclaimed. "I thought 'twas the old lord himself when first you spoke. Flay the skin off you with his tongue, so he could, cleaner than most men'd do it with a horsewhip. And you're his very moral. You should watch it, you know. It's a damned unpleasant trick and may lose you a good friend."

"Since my ambition falls short of aspiring to friendship with such as you, the thought does not unduly depress me," said Robert suavely. "I would, however, be interested to hear your explanation of tonight's activities."

O'Malley appeared to reflect for a moment or two, then heaved a resigned sigh. "Since you are so insistent," he conceded, glancing sadly at his bonds. "Though I find it hard to forgive your unwarrantable interference in as neat a scheme as ever a man could wish for. Had you but let well alone, *you* might both be sleeping comfortably in your beds and *I* should have been securely established for life."

Had it not been for his knowledge of an earlier 'neat scheme' conceived by this same ingenious rascal, Robert might have found it in him to smile at the fellow's consummate impudence. As it was, he said impatiently, "You talk too much, and nothing to the point. Cut line."

O'Malley managed to lever himself on to one elbow and regarded him reproachfully. "No. I see that you are not the man to appreciate subtlety. Very well, then. I will make all plain. Have you examined the poniard that I saw you set down on the ledge there? Did you not think it a strange weapon to choose for such a task as you thought me engaged upon? Not only is it quite unique. It is designed for stabbing rather than for slashing. Would *you* choose such a tool if you planned to hamstring a horse? Not, of course, that you would entertain any such dastardly notion, any more that I would myself," he threw in hastily, seeing Robert's expression. "But pray show it to Mr. Hornby. I think I may depend upon his recognition of the piece."

The recognition was patent. Brandon's eyes widened a little, but he only said quietly, "Yes. I know it well."

"To confess to Lord Finmore that I had lost a dagger

that anyone familiar with Finmore House would readily recognise, when disturbed in my approach by a wakeful groom would, I felt, cause him to feel a considerable degree of alarm. He would certainly be willing to pay me a handsome sum to acknowledge my personal guilt by fleeing the country. And since I have felt for some time that my talents were wasted in my present limited sphere, such an arrangement would suit me very well. If his offer was sufficiently substantial I would be prepared to accept it. You now have the truth of the matter."

"Some of it," said Brandon sceptically. "Never tell me you thought to frighten Lord Finmore with such a taradiddle! He's not such a fool. He's but to say the thing had been taken without his knowledge—and his word would be believed before yours. No. You've more against him than *that*."

For the first time O'Malley looked less than well pleased with himself. He shrugged—as far as the rope lashings permitted—and relapsed into sulky silence.

"I'll take a look at his papers," said Robert briskly. "Though surely Wilfred wouldn't be such a fool as to put anything incriminating into writing."

To do Wilfred justice the letter, in itself, was capable of a perfectly innocent interpretation. Perhaps the most suspicious thing about it was the injunction to O'Malley in the closing sentence to burn it as soon as he had mastered its contents. It instructed him to return to Ireland as soon as he had 'completed his task'. The balance of the agreed sum would be paid to him there. On no account was he to go anywhere near London or the writer, who signed himself only with a large flourishing 'F'.

Taken in conjunction with the discovery of the poniard—the thing was centuries old and was reputed to have been brought back from Damascus by a crusading Finmore—one could see that it afforded a substantial foundation on which to base an attempt at blackmail. Small wonder that O'Malley had selected the weapon with care and had gone to such pains to plant it in a suitably prominent position.

It also furnished Robert and Brandon with precisely the sort of evidence that they needed in order to safeguard Francesca and Merlin from further threats. Their eyes met and they smiled at one another comfortably. Even towards the unwitting instrument of their relief, Robert's sentiments mellowed a little.

"And you just let him go?" demanded Francesca incredulously.

Robert looked faintly guilty. "What else could we have done with him? If we had handed him over to the law on a charge of breaking into the stables, the whole tale must have come out. And though it might have been a fitting punishment for Wilfred I cannot think that you would have wished Uncle Miles's name to be soiled with that sort of scandal." He read the agreement in her eyes and went on cheerfully, "So we sent him on his way to Town to try out his little scheme. I must say that his swollen jaw adds a convincing touch of verisimilitude to the tale." He grinned. "I daresay my precious cousin will bleed pretty freely. I certainly hope he does. Why should *he* go scot free when all the rest of us have suffered? Besides, it will be much more comfortable for you to know that O'Malley is safely out of the country—and only poetic justice that Wilfred should defray the cost of that comfort. You would not care to be for ever meeting the fellow at parties, would you?"

She smiled a little for the comical notion but said soberly, "What is he like, now? Hugh O'Malley?"

"Still handsome—impudent—plausible—much as you described him to me," returned Robert promptly. "And about as unstable as water. For the last four or five years he has been managing a stud quite close to Finmore. That was how he came to know of Merlin's existence and praised the colt so high to Wilfred that nothing would do for his lordship but to come and see for himself. He hoped to claim him as part of the Finmore stud but Uncle Miles had taken good care to guard against that. As for O'Malley, Brandon says he was going on quite prosperously in a modest way. His employers thought highly of him. But he is not the man to be content for long with steady work and hum-drum comfort. Not even his genuine love for horses could hold him to it. No need to grieve for him, love. He is the born adventurer, happiest when he is foot-loose, taking his pleasure in matching his wits against the world."

"Grieve for him? How could you suppose it? Why— I never liked him above half when I was no more than a foolish child. And how could I like him now? Think of Reyna!"

"Ah! No. On that count you must acquit him. Brandon challenged him with it—and his indignation almost matched your own. 'What! Me?' he said. 'Poison a vixen in the breeding season? And me as keen a hunting man as ever came out of Ireland!' I believed him. We both did. Maybe it was the truest word he spoke.

I doubt we shall never know who Wilfred suborned to play that nasty trick—but I'll take my oath it wasn't O'Malley. In fact, he made a bad mistake when he tried to bribe O'Malley to hamstring the colt."

She looked at him curiously. "I think you value him more highly than I do," she said quietly.

He smiled at her. "Think a moment, my girl. Have I not good cause? I'll confess that last night I detested him right heartily. It would have given me considerable satisfaction to administer the thrashing that he certainly deserved—if only," he put in teasingly, "because of the sleep he'd caused me to lose. But though I can never forgive him for the unhappiness that he brought upon you in the past, yet I do owe him gratitude on two counts. His intervention in the Merlin affair has provided us with just the evidence we needed to make dear Cousin Wilfred behave himself—and *how* I shall enjoy writing to inform him that not only the dagger but his letter, too, are in *my* keeping and not, after all, in O'Malley's!"

He contemplated this pleasing thought with obvious satisfaction until Francesca said, "And the second count?"

"If he had not made off with you and so, quite by accident, I admit, brought you under my uncle's protection, we might never have met," he said simply, and took her hand to draw her gently into his arms. He looked down at her, resting so confidingly in his hold, and said, the more lightly because of the very depth of his love for her, "Just think of it! In your first season you would undoubtedly have made a brilliant match. Instead of gypsying all over Europe and acquiring a number of vastly unfeminine tricks, you would now be a meek and dutiful wife and the mother of a large and lively family." He considered her pensively, then sighed and shook his head. "Alas, no! Meek and dutiful I fear you will never be. It is far too late to mend your ways. But as for the family, now that is a different matter. Do you think we might do something about that?"

Under his smiling gaze Francesca blushed scarlet, to her own fury. Her head went up with a pretty assumption of dignity. "Indeed, sir!" she said innocently. "Are we then to be wed? Is it not usual to ask the lady's consent before proceeding quite so far with your plans?"

There could be only one answer to that sort of thing. The arms that had been holding her so gently hardened and tightened until she gasped for breath. "No. Definitely not meek and dutiful," said Robert thoughtfully, and kissed her long and fiercely until the pretence of defiance melted into loving submission, until he felt the growing response in the soft mouth beneath his own, the pliant body that clung, and knew, guiltily but triumphantly, that she would yield herself to him then and there if he required it of her. Only then did he hold her a little away from him and softly repeat her own words. "*Are* we then to be wed, my love? I had thought the question both asked and answered when I held you in my arms before. But it seems that I did not make myself sufficiently plain. And it is only right that you should understand the manner of marriage I have in mind. No fashionable marriage of convenience for us, my darling, with both of us free to go our own ways so long as due propriety is observed. Once we are married I will not willingly let you out of my sight again. We have wasted too much time already. You shall come adventuring abroad with me if the fancy takes us. You shall go to all the parties that your young heart ached for. But always we will come home together to Saxondene and, please God, to our children. Now—answer me, as your heart bids you."

She looked back at him, her eyes wide and dark with the glory and the wonder of love that he had permitted her to glimpse. "When you will, beloved," she said simply. "Life can offer me no greater joy than that it should be shared with you."

His kiss was gentler this time, the strong arms that held her protective rather than masterful. "Then we'll be married as soon as I can obtain a licence," he said. "Here? In the village church? Or would you prefer to be married from your aunt's house in Town?"

She pulled a wry face at the very suggestion. "Here, please, with Mr. Whittingham to marry us. And Robin can be my bride's maiden. I hope Robin will like it— our marrying. I will try very hard to be a good Mama to her," she told him solemnly.

He chuckled and pinched her cheek. "Small doubt of that. But don't show me such a sober face over it. If you imagine that I'm marrying you to provide Robin with a step-mama, you're fair and far off! As for her liking it—well, I believe she does still sleep at home, and she usually favours me with her company at breakfast and at dinner, but whenever I enquire for her I am invariably told that she has 'just run down to South Gates' or is 'out riding with Miss Thornish'. So I should think it will save her a good deal of trouble to have us residing under the same roof. And speaking of South Gates, what will you do with it when we marry? Make it over to Brandon and Cathy?"

"But I forfeit South Gates if I marry. Don't you remember? By the terms of your uncle's will it reverts to you—though it will cost you a handsome marriage portion!" Her eyes lit with mischief. "Ah! But of course. Now I see it all. *That* is why you managed to bring yourself at last to offer for me. In doing so you secure both South Gates *and* the money." She took care to effect a rapid retreat as she said it and adopted a strategic position at the opposite end of the library table, adding for good measure, "Even an ageing spinster will 'go off' you see, so the dowry be sufficient to sweeten the dose!"

The golden eyes were laughing at him. Across the six foot breadth of oak it seemed safe enough to venture such outrageous provocation. He was in no position to retaliate.

But she had underestimated her adversary.

"*And* a considerable fortune in your own right," he reminded her gently, with an air of deep satisfaction. "You must remember *that*. I doubt if the other inducements you mentioned would have been sufficient."

She was so completely taken aback that she forgot to be wary, and while she stared at him open-mouthed he set a hand on the table and swung himself across to catch her swiftly by the shoulders and give her an admonitory shake.

"And that is much less than you deserve," he told her severely. "I'm half of a mind to administer the spanking that you are asking for." And he sounded so determined about it that she glanced up at his face, startled, to see if he really meant it and was quite relieved to see that he was smiling.

"Ageing spinster, indeed! I should rather say shameless baggage! But just wait until we are married, my girl. And don't say I didn't give you fair warning."

"No, dear Robert," said the shameless baggage demurely.

"And do you still wish to marry me?" demanded her future lord and master.

"Yes, please," said Miss Thornish. And then, unregenerate to the last, "More than ever."

Romantic Fiction

If you like novels of passion and daring adventure that take you to the very heart of human drama, these are the books for you.

☐ AFTER—Anderson	Q2279	1.50
☐ THE DANCE OF LOVE—Dodson	23110-0	1.75
☐ A GIFT OF ONYX—Kettle	23206-9	1.50
☐ TARA'S HEALING—Giles	23012-0	1.50
☐ THE TROIKA BELLE—Morris	23013-9	1.75
☐ THE DEFIANT DESIRE—Klem	13741-4	1.75
☐ LOVE'S TRIUMPHANT HEART—Ashton	13771-6	1.75
☐ MAJORCA—Dodson	13740-6	1.75

Buy them at your local bookstores or use this handy coupon for ordering:

Norah Lofts

Norah Lofts weaves a rich tapestry of love, war and passion.
Here are her most entertaining novels of romance and intrigue.
You may order any or all direct by mail.

☐	BRIDE OF MOAT HOUSE	22527-5	1.50
☐	THE BRITTLE GLASS	23037-6	1.75
☐	THE CONCUBINE	Q2405	1.50
☐	CROWN OF ALOES	23030-9	1.75
☐	ELEANOR THE QUEEN	Q2848	1.50
☐	THE GOLDEN FLEECE	23132-1	1.75
☐	HEAVEN IN YOUR HAND	P2451	1.25
☐	THE HOUSE AT OLD VINE	Q2494	1.50
☐	THE HOUSE AT SUNSET	Q2492	1.50
☐	JASSY	Q2711	1.50
☐	THE KING'S PLEASURE	23139-9	1.75
☐	KNIGHT'S ACRE	X2685	1.75
☐	THE LUTE PLAYER	22948-3	1.95
☐	THE LITTLE WAX DOLL	P2270	1.25
☐	THE LOST QUEEN	Q2154	1.50
☐	LOVERS ALL UNTRUE	Q2792	1.50
☐	NETHERGATE	23095-3	1.75
☐	OUT OF THE DARK	Q2762	1.50
☐	A ROSE FOR VIRTUE	X2781	1.75
☐	SCENT OF CLOVES	22977-7	1.75
☐	TO SEE A FINE LADY	22890-8	1.75
☐	THE TOWN HOUSE	X2793	1.75
☐	WINTER HARVEST	X2855	1.75

Buy them at your local bookstores or use this handy coupon for ordering:

FAWCETT PUBLICATIONS, P.O. Box 1014, Greenwich Conn. 06830

Please send me the books I have checked above. Orders for less than 5 books must include 60c for the first book and 25c for each additional book to cover mailing and handling. Orders of 5 or more books postage is Free. I enclose $_____ in check or money order.

Mr/Mrs/Miss _____

Address _____

City _____ State/Zip _____

Please allow 4 to 5 weeks for delivery. This offer expires 6/78.   A-13